"I'd neve̶̶̶̶̶̶̶̶̶̶̶̶̶̶̶̶̶̶̶̶ hurt our baby," Jenny whispered.

Her choice of words slipped like a lance of sweetness into Ned's thoughts.

Though he hadn't contributed to the miracle of life within her, the child she'd bear would belong to him. He'd nurture and care for it, love it as she did. For one blazing moment he felt as if they were the only two people in the world. He didn't want the sensation to end.

Jenny didn't either. For the first time since she could remember, she didn't feel as if she was alone in the world. Whatever Ned thought of her, she still had him.

She wished once again that she'd met Ned and not his brother first.

Dear Reader,

Warning! Don't read April's terrific lineup of Silhouette Romance titles *unless* you're ready to catch spring fever!

The FABULOUS FATHERS series continues with Suzanne Carey's *Dad Galahad*. Ned Balfour, the story's hero, is all a modern knight should be—and *more*. Ned gallantly marries pregnant Jenny McClain to give her child a name. But he never expects the powerful emotions that come with being a father. *And* Jenny's husband.

Garrett Scott, the hero of *Who's That Baby?* by Kristin Morgan, is a father with a mysterious past. He's a man on the run, determined to protect his daughter. Then Garrett meets Whitney Arceneaux, a woman whose warmth and beauty tempt him to share his secret—and his heart.

Laurie Paige's popular ALL-AMERICAN SWEETHEARTS trilogy concludes this month with a passionate battle of wills in *Victoria's Conquest*. Jason Broderick fell in love with Victoria Broderick years ago—the day she married his late cousin. Now that Victoria is free and needs help, Jason will give her just about anything she wants. Anything *but* his love.

Rounding out the list, there's the sparkling, romantic mix-up of Patricia Ellis's *Sorry, Wrong Number* and Maris Soule's delightful and moving love story, *Lyon's Pride*. One of your favorite authors, Marie Ferrarella blends just the right touch of heartfelt emotion, warmth and humor in *The Right Man*.

In the coming months, look for more books by your favorite authors, including Diana Palmer, Elizabeth August, Phyllis Halldorson and many more.

Happy reading from all of us at Silhouette!

Anne Canadeo
Senior Editor

DAD GALAHAD
Suzanne Carey

Silhouette
ROMANCE™

Published by Silhouette Books New York

America's Publisher of Contemporary Romance

For 'Old Nance,' outstanding daughter, talented writer and coadventurer, with love from her mom.

Special thanks to Lee Gilbert, and to the folks at Cunard Hotel La Toc and La Toc Suites, Castries, St. Lucia.

SILHOUETTE BOOKS
300 E. 42nd St., New York, N.Y. 10017

DAD GALAHAD

Copyright © 1993 by Verna Carey

All rights reserved. Except for use in any review, the reproduction or utilization of this work in whole or in part in any form by any electronic, mechanical or other means, now known or hereafter invented, including xerography, photocopying and recording, or in any information storage or retrieval system, is forbidden without the permission of the publisher, Silhouette Books, 300 E. 42nd St., New York, N.Y. 10017

ISBN: 0-373-08928-7

First Silhouette Books printing April 1993

All the characters in this book have no existence outside the imagination of the author and have no relation whatsoever to anyone bearing the same name or names. They are not even distantly inspired by any individual known or unknown to the author, and all incidents are pure invention.

®: Trademark used under license and registered in the United States Patent and Trademark Office and in other countries.

Printed in the U.S.A.

Books by Suzanne Carey

Silhouette Romance

A Most Convenient Marriage #633
Run, Isabella #682
Virgin Territory #736
The Baby Contract #777
Home for Thanksgiving #825
Navajo Wedding #855
Baby Swap #880
Dad Galahad #928

Silhouette Desire

Kiss and Tell #4
Passion's Portrait #69
Mountain Memory #92
Leave Me Never #126
Counterparts #176
Angel in His Arms #206
Confess to Apollo #268
Love Medicine #310
Any Pirate in a Storm #368

Silhouette Intimate Moments

Never Say Goodbye #330
Strangers When We Meet #392
True to the Fire #435

SUZANNE CAREY

is a former reporter and magazine editor who prefers
to write romance novels because they add to the sum
total of love in the world.

Ned Balfour on Fatherhood...

Just look at you, little man. An hour ago, we hadn't met. I didn't know your name. You were still an unknown quantity, inside your mother's body, getting ready to be born.

Now you're here, breathing on your own in a hospital delivery room, with the flush of your first squalls fading from your cheeks.

Where before Andrew Nicholas Balfour didn't exist, you *are*—a miniature, perfect person with dark hair and half-moons on your fingernails, the beginnings of a yawn distorting your mouth.

More than I thought possible, I love you already. I can't keep the tears from flowing as I hold you in my arms.

I'd given up hope of ever being a father. Now, though technically my brother gave you life, you're mine in every other respect.

Because I had the presence of mind to marry your mother and keep you in the family, I'll be the one to watch over your first steps and kiss the hurt from your bruises. I can't wait to talk to you. Discover how your mind works. Share your hopes and dreams.

But I don't want to hurry, son.

God, how that word catches in my throat!

Before I know it, you'll be driving your first car. Going off to university. Getting married and becoming a father yourself.

Sooner than I like to think—though I'll feel such pride when it does happen—we'll be men together.

Chapter One

"Here we are, miss," the cabby announced, braking in front of an angular concrete-and-glass building on Lime Street, not far from Lloyd's of London.

In the taxi's back seat, Seattle native Jennifer McClain didn't respond for a moment. Her fingers were cold, their knuckles white against her skin as they gripped the strap of her leather shoulder bag. Will I be able to carry this off? she wondered, longing to turn tail and run now that she was actually there, on Ned Balfour's doorstep.

Given her predicament, Jenny believed, she didn't have any other choice. Brushing back a strand of the light brown hair that in recent weeks seemed to have lost its luster, she handed over the requisite fare plus a tip she could ill afford.

Though it was May and the city's daffodils were in bloom, overnight the weather had turned chilly. She emerged from the cab in a cold, gray drizzle. Aware she looked sufficiently bedraggled without getting wet, she dashed into the glass-enclosed lobby, drawing her courage about her like a cloak.

A wave of nausea washed over her as she scanned a roster of the building's tenants. She was determined not to give in to it. No matter how rotten she felt, she couldn't afford to let her physical distress get in the way if Balfour Shipping's chief executive officer granted her an interview.

According to the roster, the firm's offices occupied the top three floors. With a little stab of bravado, Jenny summoned the lift. *If I can get through this crisis without asking for Aunt Etta's help, I'll never look at another man,* she promised herself, *let alone give one the chance to take advantage of my stupidity and naiveté.*

The secretary stationed outside Ned Balfour's office was middle-aged, elegant in gray wool jersey and silver bracelets, clearly a guardian at the gate. "Yes?" she inquired in her frosty upper-class British accent.

Jenny drew herself up to her full five-foot-six-inch height. "Mr. Balfour, please."

The woman regarded her doubtfully. "Do you have an appointment?"

"No, but..."

"Then I'm afraid he can't see you, miss. He has an exceptionally busy schedule this week."

Jenny's lower lip trembled. For the past several months, her emotions had run perilously close to the surface. *I refuse to behave like an object of pity,* she thought. *I'm not here for a free ride. If Milo's brother is willing to advance the money I need, I'll repay every penny.*

Apparently something in her demeanor caused the secretary to take a second look. "Perhaps if you could state your business..." she said somewhat more kindly.

Jenny blinked back a tear that threatened to spill. How could she confess her plight to this sleek, composed stranger who'd probably never been guilty of a serious misstep.

"I'm a friend of Milo's," she said miserably. "My purpose in asking to see Mr. Balfour is...rather personal. If you could possibly ask..."

To her surprise, the woman relented almost at once. "Hold on half a moment," she murmured. "I'll see if there's anything I can do."

At the oversize desk of exquisitely carved West Indian mahogany where his father had presided as chairman of the board until a heart attack had slowed him down a few months earlier, thirty-nine-year-old Ned Balfour was whittling away at a stack of papers, all of them in need of his immediate attention. He had a mountain of work facing him before he left for St. Lucia, and more would accumulate in his absence. Thank God he had an able, trustworthy assistant in Nigel Carstairs. He couldn't count on Milo for any help.

The scowl that drew his dark brows together deepened slightly when his intercom buzzed, disrupting his concentration. "Mrs. Phipps," he accused in his raspy bass, "I thought I told you I wasn't to be disturbed."

The secretary's apology was smooth, with an undertone of confidence that bespoke her many years' service with the firm. "Indeed you did, Mr. Balfour," she confessed. "But there's a young lady out here who says she's a friend of your brother's. She seems to feel it's urgent that she speak with you."

Taking off his horn-rimmed reading glasses and rubbing his eyes, Ned stared at the splendid, gilt-framed Hockney that offered such a pleasing contrast to some of the family's more valuable antiques, and the faded but priceless Heriz carpet beneath his feet. So Milo had done it again, damn him. He'd be expected to pick up the pieces as before.

"All right...show her in," he said, getting to his feet.

The woman Liz Phipps ushered into his office was reed-slender and very young—twenty-two or thereabouts, Ned guessed. Her light brown hair was dullish and damp from the rain. Several strands had worked loose from an Edwardian-style knot to hang limply around her face. Yet there was something inherently appealing about her. She didn't look as if she were feeling well.

"Please sit down," he said, steeling himself not to have too much sympathy for her. "Shall I ask Mrs. Phipps to fetch us some tea?"

Dumfounded that gaining his ear had been so easy, Jenny didn't remove her loosely belted beige raincoat. "No, thank you," she said in a small voice, her accent revealing her to be an American as she sank into a dark blue velvet chair opposite his desk.

Ned dismissed his secretary with a nod. The rich leather of his armchair creaked faintly as he retook his seat. "So," he prompted, wishing he couldn't predict the path their conversation would take, "Mrs. Phipps tells me you're a friend of my brother's. What can I do for you?"

Jenny hadn't felt so tongue-tied since she was a child. In part, she knew, her nervousness stemmed from the purpose of her visit. She suspected it also had something to do with the man himself.

He wasn't at all like Milo. But then the incorrigible playboy who bore at least half the responsibility for her predicament had told her as much. "Ned's all business...a regular stick-in-the-mud," he'd claimed.

Older, darker and far more serious-looking than his carefree sibling, Ned Balfour had failed to attain Milo's six-foot, two-inch height by several inches. He wasn't handsome in a conventional sense. Yet he was far from ordinary. Though he might not have his brother's easygoing charm, he radiated the kind of low-key but intense personal magnetism that could fill a room. There was a coiled tension in his compact, muscular body, a bluntness that matched his straight, somewhat abbreviated nose and slightly disparaging mouth. Jenny sensed an ability to make lightning-quick decisions that would be as flawless in a business sense as his custom-made suit and snowy shirt.

He wouldn't be an easy mark. Somehow she had to make herself ask him for money.

"Milo and I..." she began, uncertain how to proceed.

In response, one of his dark brows lifted slightly. The brown eyes that drilled into hers contained irony and a hint of regret.

He *knows,* she realized with a flood of anguish. He's been through this with one of Milo's girls before.

"I'm pregnant," she whispered as if asking forgiveness of a father confessor.

She couldn't bring herself to tell him everything. Even to her, the tale of too much champagne and her susceptibility to alcohol sounded pathetic. At twenty-six, she should have known better than to let Milo lure her into bed despite her inexperience.

"He doesn't plan to marry me," she added, deeply embarrassed. "Or offer me any assistance. When I told him what had happened, he informed me he was engaged to someone else. He said he'd try to help financially. Now he claims to have gambling debts... that he's perpetually short of funds."

Accurate on both counts, Ned thought. Having justly earned his reputation as a ruthless business-man, he saw his brother's impending marriage to Pam Fitzherbert, daughter of the firm's third-largest stockholder and sole heiress to the Fitzherbert family's extensive banana plantations on St. Lucia, in strictly financial terms. Both Milo and Pam were ir-redeemably selfish. Both would continue to play the field while extracting the maximum profit from the consolidation of assets their marriage would bring about.

Meanwhile, Balfour Shipping, which did a thriving business importing tropical fruits, was on the verge of major expansion in several areas. Though the firm had a solid capital base and the family's fortune was healthy, to say the least, Ned didn't see any reason not to keep the Fitzherbert money and bananas in his hip pocket. I'd be a fool to insist Milo break with the Fitzherberts simply to accommodate a fortune hunter, he thought. It wouldn't surprise me to learn she got herself pregnant so he'd have to marry her.

"Why come to me?" he asked, thrusting the onus of solving her problem back at her while keeping his general distrust of women to himself. "I can't believe you expect me to pressure Milo on your behalf. Or reward you with cash for threats of a paternity suit."

She blanched. "Certainly not! Such a suit never occurred to me."

To her credit, she hadn't mentioned the newspapers. Of course, that might indicate she was a skilled negotiator, with a trump card up her sleeve. If she was playacting the innocent, she was doing a damn fine job of it.

Tilting his head to one side, he regarded her in silence for a moment. "Yet I *am* correct in assuming you need money," he observed, phrasing the statement as a question.

Incredibly he planned to make things easy for her.

"I'm ashamed to admit it. But you're right," she acknowledged with a surge of gratitude. "You see, I gave up my job as a kindergarten teacher...cashed in my savings to come here and train with Nannies, Ltd. After getting a little field experience, I planned to start a similar business in Seattle. There's an excellent market..."

"And now?"

"Now, I'm sick...queasy twenty-four hours a day. Some mornings it's all I can do to drag myself out of bed. In the hope of working out something with Milo, I let my return ticket lapse. I'm dangerously short of funds. I need enough money to get back to the States... *and* something to live on until I can arrange..."

About to tell him of her intention to apply for public aid until she felt well enough to take on some kind of work, she decided against it. If he agreed to lend her the money she needed, she'd return every cent. Her future plans were none of his affair.

Ned contemplated her unfinished revelation with distaste. She hadn't come right out and said so. Yet he suspected the forlorn Miss McClain planned to spend part of any money he gave her on a swift medical procedure to relieve her of her burden. Though he disapproved, he didn't feel his opinion should be allowed to matter. He wasn't the baby's father. He didn't have the right to interfere.

"Surely you have relatives to whom you can turn for help," he suggested.

She shook her head. "There isn't anyone."

That wasn't strictly true, of course. Etta Nelson, the elderly great-aunt who'd raised her after her father's disappearance and mother's death, possessed the means to offer her financial assistance. But the prospect of asking her wasn't sweet. Unless the small, innocent being inside her would be harmed in some way by doing without Aunt Etta's charity, Jenny hoped to sidestep her scorn and condemnation.

Whatever her plans, if Milo had gotten her pregnant, she deserved some sort of help, Ned decided. He might as well be generous. His time was limited, and it would save them both a great deal of unpleasantness. Suppressing a sigh, he withdrew a large old-fashioned checkbook from the center drawer of his desk. "Ten thousand ought to cover things," he said, unable to keep a strong note of displeasure from his voice. "Translated to dollars, that's roughly seventeen thousand dollars. More than enough for seven months' living expenses. And an abortion..."

Jenny leapt to her feet, her green eyes blazing. "I don't plan to get one!" she gasped.

If he didn't do something to prevent it, she'd storm out of his office and catch a cab to Fleet Street. The

Balfour name would be dragged through the mud of the morning papers. With a sudden display of agility, Ned circumnavigated his desk to place a restraining hand on her sleeve.

To Jenny's chagrin, she found herself noticing the crisp scent of his after-shave. She'd never seen such thick, dark lashes. Or such an expressive mouth.

"Miss...er, McClain, is it?" he asked in the deep-pitched voice that had begun to send little shivers racing down her arms. "Please don't go. I'm sorry I offended you. Naturally I assumed..."

"You had no right to assume anything."

Still skeptical, he gave her full marks as a negotiator. "Please accept my apology," he said, his fingers relaxing their hold though it was clear he didn't plan to let her slip away from him just yet. "It seems I judged you too harshly. In my own defense, I do have a peripheral interest..."

Still quivering with outrage, Jenny didn't believe his protestation of personal concern for a moment. In her opinion, his only desire was to get rid of her as quickly as possible, no matter what the cost.

"I trust the baby you're carrying *is* Milo's," he added softly, deliberately provoking her so he could gauge her reaction. "That it couldn't have been fathered by another man...."

At the none-too-subtle suggestion she might be promiscuous, Jenny's fury knew no bounds. "I don't have to stay here and listen to this!" she exclaimed, attempting to wrench free of him. "If I have to, I'll sign my baby over to adoptive parents *before* it's born. At least that way he or she won't start life sick or retarded due to the lack of proper nutrition!"

Stunned, Ned somehow kept his feelings from altering his composure. He didn't relinquish his hold on her. "You mean..."

"Support for unwed mothers willing to sign away their rights in a private adoption proceeding is readily available in the United States. I expect it wouldn't be too difficult to make similar arrangements here in England."

He didn't reply and again she tried to free herself, to no avail. "If you don't let me go, Mr. Balfour," she added softly, "I'm going to scream."

She was planning to carry her child to term. Burned as he'd been by a gold digger who'd been careful not to get pregnant so she could cheat on him with impunity, something softened in Ned's face.

"Have you seen a doctor?" he asked.

His abruptly compassionate tone threw her for a loop. "Once right after I began to suspect," she answered, feeling as if her legs wouldn't hold her. "I don't have insurance and, at that time, I'd only been in England two months. I wasn't eligible for free medical care except in an emergency. When I hit the three-month mark in April, I began...visiting a clinic regularly...."

Her voice trailed off, as if from sudden weakness. Though they were strangers, one of Ned's strong arms found its way around her shoulders. "I *am* going to ring for tea," he decided. "If you'll sit down and talk with me a little further, Miss McClain, I promise I won't insult you again."

Her knees about to buckle, Jenny didn't feel as if she could refuse him. "All right," she conceded. "But if you so much as suggest..."

The corners of his mouth turned down slightly. "You have my word."

Mrs. Phipps brought the tea in Minton cups on a silver tray. It was accompanied by a selection of what the British fondly termed "biscuits." To her surprise, Jenny was suddenly ravenous.

For several minutes they partook in silence, with Ned seated in the companion chair to hers and the tea tray resting on a low table between them. Beyond his dramatic wall of windows, they could see the Thames's leaden glint through the city haze. It had stopped raining, at least temporarily. A late-afternoon mist was beginning to curl around Tower Bridge.

"Tell me something about yourself," he requested.

It seemed an odd thing to ask, given the fact that, once she had the price of a plane ticket, they'd never see each other again. She decided to humor him. Not quite meeting his eyes, she recited the basic facts, beginning with her birth and continuing through college to her most recent job with the King County public school system.

She had a middle-American, churchgoing background. And she was educated. "Boyfriends? Husbands?" he asked.

Jenny tried to ignore the intrusiveness of his gaze. "A few of the former," she said. "I've never been married, though."

"Yet, like most women, you probably want to be."

To her, his comment sounded like a dig. "I thought so once," she murmured, deciding not to take offense. "I no longer feel that way."

She'd been burned, too. Or so she wanted him to believe. Was it possible they had interests in common? Unbidden, an off-the-wall idea crept into his thoughts.

First in his class at the London School of Economics, Ned hadn't earned his reputation for shrewdness and creativity by shunning unorthodox decision-making. "If you don't mind, Miss McClain," he said slowly, allowing himself to play with the notion that had occurred to him as if he were juggling a live grenade, "I'd like a little time to consider what should be done in your situation. Meanwhile, perhaps you'd be willing to see our family physician at my expense. Mrs. Phipps can arrange an appointment for you. How does tomorrow afternoon sound?"

Apparently he wanted to authenticate her pregnancy. If so, she couldn't blame him. Yet how could she prove... Abandoning such questions as impossible of resolution, she agreed to do as he asked.

"I'll get back to you as soon as you've had your exam," he promised, taking down her address and phone number before seeing her to the door of his office and bidding her farewell with a perfunctory handshake. "Thursday, at the latest."

Like that of his nearness, the effect of Ned's touch was electric. Jenny was flooded with shame. In her condition, she had no business being attracted to anyone, least of all a tough, practical business executive who doubted her credibility and happened to be Milo's brother.

Jenny's visit to Dr. Woolsey the following afternoon was uneventful but immensely reassuring. Despite her day-long bouts with "morning sickness," he told her she was healthy. To all indications, her baby was doing well.

"Three months along, I should think," he said, confirming what she already knew. "What's needed at the moment is rest, moderate exercise, good, wholesome food and a complete lack of stress. Before long, your body should adjust."

As she left his office a few minutes later, Jenny felt the first measure of peace that had permeated her soul since she'd learned she was pregnant. Her unremitting nausea had worried her. Now she knew both she and the baby were all right. And, though she was convinced Ned Balfour was primarily concerned with profit and loss, not good works, she had the feeling he intended to help her. Dipping into her slender reserve of cash on the way home to her Chelsea bed-sitting room, she celebrated by buying oranges and chocolates.

Seated in his leather chair later that afternoon and staring out his expansive wall of windows, Ned listened on his speaker phone to the preliminary report of a private detective he'd hired to check on Jenny. It seemed there wasn't much to tell. Though she had to have slept with his brother at least once in order to be carrying his child, the dour investigator who'd previously worked for Scotland Yard hadn't turned up any evidence of promiscuity on her part.

Though for several weeks she'd spent considerable time in Milo's company, sight-seeing, dining out and attending the theater, there were no telltale records of weekends in the country—merely corroboration from Milo's neighbors that she'd paid a single visit to his flat.

"The word from Seattle is that her social life there was modest to a fault," the detective concluded. "Do you want the details, Mr. Balfour? There aren't many."

"No, that's all right," Ned answered. "Thanks for the prompt service. I trust you'll send us a bill?"

Flipping his phone switch to Off, he stared meditatively at the Hockney for a moment. Jennifer McClain's amazingly uncheckered past was pushing him in a direction he wasn't sure he ought to go. It was time to check with Ian Woolsey.

As expected, Ned's family doctor and friend confirmed Jenny's pregnancy. From a physical standpoint, everything appeared to be going well. She was due to give birth the final week in November.

There was a pause in the conversation. Sensing a moment of indecision on his friend's part, Ned didn't speak.

"Tell me I'm out of line if you like," Ian Woolsey said at last. "But Miss McClain seems a proper young lady. I can't help wondering whether the child she's carrying is Milo's. Or..."

The unspoken implication that *he* might have fathered the baby in question amused and saddened Ned. Though he'd sown plenty of wild oats in his youth, since catching Ronnie in bed with his charming, good-for-nothing brother four years earlier, he'd sidestepped involvement with the opposite sex. For the most part, he'd buried himself in his work—the selfsame activity his ex-wife had cited as an excuse for her faithlessness.

A career-oriented television personality who'd enjoyed spending his money while carefully banking her own, Veronica Partridge Balfour hadn't wanted children. Unwilling to subject himself to marriage again, Ned had been forced to come to terms with the likelihood he'd never be a father. Now Milo had a baby on the way—one he didn't want. The situation had touched a nerve.

During the past twenty-four hours, he'd given it a lot of thought. Thanks to the detective's report, he was inclined to proceed with the idea that had occurred to him. There were loose ends, of course. He didn't have a clue whether Jennifer McClain had been in love with his brother or simply interested in snagging a wealthy husband when the two of them had gone to bed. Either way, the thought of being associated with another of Milo's conquests wasn't terribly appealing to Ned. He supposed it wouldn't make any difference, given the parameters he had in mind.

At the other end of the phone connection, Ian Woolsey was waiting.

"Let's just say Miss McClain's baby will be a Balfour," Ned told him at last. "Don't worry, Ian. I'll see to it she's well provided for."

Jenny was asleep by the time Ned phoned. Struggling awake at her landlady's knock, she padded downstairs in her robe and slippers to take his call.

"As I'm sure Ian told you," he said without preamble when she greeted him, "you're doing fine. So is your baby. Would it be possible for us to meet tomorrow afternoon, say around 4:00 p.m., in order to continue our discussion?"

What else is there to talk about? Jenny wondered. We've covered everything. Over the phone, she had no way of reading him. "I suppose so," she agreed after a moment.

"Good." His raspy bass held a distinct note of satisfaction. "I'll send my car for you around four, then. Sleep well."

The arrival of Ned's chauffeur-driven Bentley caused Jenny's landlady to twitch back the curtains. They didn't head for Lime Street and the offices of Balfour Shipping as Jenny expected. Instead they turned down St. Katherine's West, between Tower Bridge and the renovated dock area beside the river. Once again, it was raining—this time with some earnestness.

"Mr. Balfour instructed me to wait here for him, miss," the chauffeur said, pulling over into a parking stall. "If you'd like tea, I have a thermos."

Jenny declined with thanks. She felt out of her element, consigned to limbo in the unfamiliar Bentley as she waited for a man she barely knew. Her thoughts going nowhere, like laboratory mice on a researcher's treadmill, she stared at the forest of pleasure-boat masts that bobbed in the marina below tall brick warehouses that had been converted to chic apartments. Did Ned Balfour plan to lend her the money she needed? Or didn't he? She'd begun to entertain a sinking feeling he had something completely different in mind.

Abruptly one of the Bentley's rear doors opened and he got in beside her. To her astonishment, he'd been jogging despite the inclement weather. His gray sweats were drenched, his dark hair plastered to his forehead.

He gave the latter a quick rubdown with a hand towel he carried inside his zippered top. "The yacht, I think, Ryerson," he told the chauffeur, nodding a brisk greeting to her. "Most of the flat's already dust-covered in anticipation of my trip."

As before, his magnetism was an all-but-tangible thing. Though she was pregnant with his brother's child and she couldn't honestly say she liked him, Jenny wasn't immune. There was something danger-ously alluring about him. He was unpredictable, like a wild animal. She half expected him to shake the wa-ter droplets that clung to him in her face.

His yacht was a double-masted sloop, gleaming with brass fittings and teak cabinetry. Dismissing the chauffeur with instructions to return in an hour, Ned helped her board and put the kettle on himself.

"Make yourself comfortable, Miss McClain," he invited, waving her to a built-in sofa with nubby tweed cushion covers before disappearing into an adjoining cabin to change.

He didn't bother to shut the door. As she waited for him, listening to the halyards creak and the rain beat against canvas and metal fittings, Jenny tried not to notice the yacht's gentle swaying. Perhaps because her stress had been alleviated by Ian Woolsey's reassur-ance that she was doing well and the renewed hope that she might be going home soon, her nausea had lessened. She didn't want it to return with a ven-geance, particularly not in Ned Balfour's presence.

Seconds later, the unsettled state of her digestive tract was the furthest thing from her head. Aided by a serendipitous juxtaposition of mirrors resulting from the partially open cabin door, she glimpsed a scene she would never forget. Stripped of his running suit, Mi-lo's older brother stood naked beside his double bunk, rubbing down vigorously with a monogrammed bath towel.

Finished, he dropped it to reach for a navy blue
terry robe. His unadorned body was magnificent—a
ripple of well-defined torso muscles flowing into lean
hips and taut buttocks. Though she had scant experience in such matters, Jenny realized he was very well
endowed.

He chose that moment to glance in the mirror he
was facing. Their gazes met at a remove, brown eyes
searing green until it seemed spontaneous combus-
tion must result. Jenny could feel herself blushing
scarlet.

She couldn't look at him when, clad in the robe with
its tie securely fastened around his waist, he came out
a moment later to make tea for them.

For his part, Ned was awash in conflicting emotions. When their gazes had fused in the mirrors that
way, she'd looked so furious and helpless—almost as
if she hadn't seen a naked man before.

Though he couldn't put his feelings into words, he
knew the fallout was considerable. Instead of regard-
ing her as a vessel that contained an infant related to
him, he'd begun to view her as a woman. It didn't
bode well for the radical but disinterested solution he
was about to propose.

Chapter Two

From Jenny's perspective, the yacht's main cabin, spacious for a sloop of its class but in reality not very large, shrank to uncomfortably small proportions when Ned handed her a steaming mug of tea and settled in a built-in lounge chair catty-corner to her. Thanks to the compact seating arrangement, his knees were almost touching hers. She was painfully aware of the hard physique beneath the folds of his dark blue terry robe.

The power of his keen, intrusive gaze made her nervous, too. Apparently as a precondition to lending her the money she needed, he considered himself justified in examining every nook and cranny of her soul.

"Have you considered keeping the baby?" he asked abruptly, putting her still further on the defensive.

Two days earlier, he'd been ready to pay for an abortion, if that's what she'd wanted. Now it seemed he was taking the opposite tack. I don't like answer-

ing to him for òne of the most painful decisions I've
ever had to make, she thought. He's a stranger, even
if he is Milo's brother. Yet it was clear that if she
wanted him to help her, she had to cooperate.

"Yes, I have," she replied, forcing herself to bare
her feelings. "I'll admit that, when I first found out I
was pregnant, I felt trapped. I wished with all my heart
that the 'mistake' I'd made would unmake itself.
Gradually, though, I began to think of the baby as a
person . . . to care about it and realize it deserved a life
of its own. I began to imagine myself as its
mother . . . cuddling it in my arms."

The poignant glimpse she'd offered of her emotions evoked a gut-level response from Ned. Determined not to be taken in by her, he resisted it. At
worst, she was an opportunist who'd fallen victim to
her own scheming—at best a fool and casual with her
favors despite the detective's report. She'd been attracted to Milo, hadn't she? Let him take her to bed?

Despite his negative feelings about her and women
in general, she'd made a favorable impression on him.
She had regular features. Good manners. And a college degree. According to Ian Woolsey, she was
healthy, if a bit too thin. Thrust into the role against
her will, she might make a good mother. Huddled in
a loose, cranberry-colored sweater and faded jeans as
if they represented some kind of security blanket to
her, she didn't seem hopelessly self-absorbed.

He framed his mug with powerful, beautifully
shaped hands. "You paint a touching picture of maternal devotion, Miss McClain," he said. "Isn't it
somewhat at odds with your plan to offer your child
for private, fee-based adoption? Or did I misunderstand you the other day?"

The last thing Jenny wanted was to give up her baby. When the time came, she knew, she'd be wrenched body from soul. She just didn't see any alternative.

"No . . . you didn't misunderstand," she admitted.

"Mind elaborating?"

How could she explain without telling Milo's disparaging, self-contained brother about the pathos of her childhood? Despite his bachelor ways, he was part of an extended family. He'd never understand the sense of deprivation she'd felt as an eight-year-old whose mother had died and whose father had left her in the lurch. Strict, undemonstrative Aunt Etta had been her only refuge.

Because of that experience, she wanted the child she carried to have all the advantages of two parents.

All the love.

"As I told you the other day, I've been feeling too rocky to work even if I could find a teaching job in my condition," she said. "Yet I need money for food and medical care. If I don't get them, my baby will suffer. Adoptive parents, carefully chosen in advance, could ease that strain for us."

Instinct argued her lack of funds was only one of several reasons she was considering the adoption route. Maybe she thought a baby would impede her business plans.

"As you say, you described your financial concerns to me the first time we met," he said with a shrug. "I'm aware they're genuine. But isn't adoption a fairly drastic step to take if you'd prefer to keep your child?"

Jenny rested one hand on the slight bulge of her stomach as if to assure the new life growing inside her that everything would be okay. "I suppose so," she admitted. "But if your resources are dwindling and there's no way to replenish them..."

The instinctive, protective gesture wasn't lost on him. "Money problems can be solved," he said brusquely. "But they aren't your only consideration. *Are* they?"

Sighing, she hoped he'd understand. "No, they're not," she admitted. "Maybe because I didn't grow up in one, I feel very strongly that children do best in a two-parent family. Much as I cherish him or her already, I'm in no position to offer this little one the security and happiness inherent in that type of situation. It's not likely I'll ever be able to offer it."

Apparently she'd meant it when she'd declared she was no longer interested in getting married someday. No doubt she's disillusioned with men, Ned thought. Under the circumstances, who can blame her?

It was ironic how closely her sentiments matched his own. Like her, he knew what it was to be burned and wary of commitment. The day he'd caught Ronnie in bed with his brother, he'd built a wall around his heart.

Yet he wanted a child. Like Jennifer McClain, he believed children deserved the love and affection of two parents. Maybe in the interest of keeping her baby she could bring herself to accept the only kind of marriage he could offer anyone.

"Supposing a way could be found for you to keep your baby," he said. "One that would guarantee him or her a secure home and the loving guidance of two parents, yet pose none of the emotional risks you'd prefer to avoid. Would you consider it?"

To Jenny's knowledge, no such way existed. Yet her heart beat faster at the possibility.

"I suppose I would," she answered slowly. "But..."

He didn't give her the chance to mount a litany of objections. "Like you, Miss McClain," he revealed, "I'm a loser at the game of love. I have no intention of falling prey to its perverse malady again. Yet I've always regretted not having a son or daughter of my own. Imagine my frustration when a young woman shows up at my office and announces she's expecting my brother's baby... adding that, since he has no interest in the child, she plans to give it up to strangers."

Put that way, the only solution she'd been able to envision sounded callous in the extreme. As for Milo's brother losing at love, she found that difficult to believe. He might not be the handsomest of men in a classical sense. But he was as wealthy as Croesus, or so Milo said. And he radiated a powerful aura of sex appeal.

For the purpose of argument, she decided to ignore her sensitivities and take him at his word. "In your place, I suppose, I'd feel life was unfair," she conceded after a moment. "I know I'd regret losing the opportunity to know my niece or nephew."

Ned nodded approvingly.

"While I may not hold Milo in particularly high regard," he confided, "we have the same parents and grandparents. The genes he contributed to your child are, therefore, very similar to my own."

It was an argument for caring about what happened, she supposed. "You're not hinting *you* want to adopt my baby, are you?" she blurted, the idea suddenly occurring to her. "Because that wouldn't allow..."

The forceful chief of Balfour Shipping regarded her steadily from beneath dark, fringed lashes. "Not exactly," he replied. "I'm asking you to marry me...on *my* terms."

If a pin had dropped in the yacht's sleekly appointed cabin just then, it would have crashed to the floor like breaking statuary. For several seconds, the only audible sounds were those of Jenny's sharply indrawn breath and the steady tattoo of the rain.

"I can't...believe you're serious," she said at last, her pupils dilating to pools of velvet.

Ned's robe gaped open slightly at the neck, offering her a glimpse of the dark chest hair she'd seen earlier. "I assure you, Miss McClain, I'm quite serious," he said.

"But we're strangers! Why should you take on a burden that rightly belongs to your brother? Even chivalry doesn't extend that far."

"I'm no Sir Galahad, if that's what you mean... sacrificing myself to aid a damsel in distress. My motives are purely selfish. As a Balfour, I want to preserve the family bloodline. I also see the chance to become a father without the emotional commitment of being a husband. A corresponding opportunity exists for you. If you choose to take it, I'll acknowledge your child as my issue, exonerating Milo of any involvement."

A second silence rested between them, fraught with possibilities. He actually means it, Jenny marveled. He'd allow the world to think he let me trap him into matrimony via unplanned parenthood. Aware of the rumors that would fly, she imagined him as her husband. A mental picture of his powerful physique, as it had been revealed to her in the juxtaposed mirrors, flashed unbidden through her head.

It was as if he could read her thoughts. "I'm not suggesting we become sex partners," he said dryly, his mouth betraying a flicker of amusement. "Merely husband and wife in a legal sense. As you say, we've just met. I realize that, given your condition and your feelings for Milo, you wouldn't find such a liaison appealing from a physical standpoint."

I don't love Milo, she contradicted him in silence. I never really did. I was swept off my feet by too much champagne and the glamour he projected.

Watching the play of emotions on her face, Ned counted it a victory that she hadn't bolted. "I mentioned terms," he reminded. "If you like, I'll be happy to enumerate them."

From Jenny's perspective, their conversation had taken on a surreal quality. This can't be happening, she thought. I'll wake up and realize I've been dreaming it.

He took her silence for assent. "What I'm suggesting is a marriage of convenience," he said. "I plan to leave next week for St. Lucia, an island near Barbados in the former British Windwards. It's business, and I may be detained there for several months. If you accept my proposal, on my return we'll share a roof though not a bed. Once the baby's born, we'll raise him or her together, as parents usually do. However, our private lives will be our own. I ask only that you be discreet in your personal dealings, and not cuckold me with my brother..."

Jenny's flush deepened. "You needn't worry about that!"

"I'm glad to hear it." Pausing, Ned searched her face. "I might add that, if you decide on another baby at some point, I shall expect to father it."

For him to talk of giving her a child when they barely knew each other and she was already pregnant with Milo's baby was almost more than she could take. "You said..."

"Surely you've heard of artificial insemination."

She didn't know how to answer him.

"I hate to sound crass," he added, "but... family assets aside... I'm fairly well fixed. Given the prevalence of divorce these days, I'll want a prenuptial contract. But you needn't worry that I plan to take advantage of you. If for some reason either of us decides we've had enough, you'll receive a handsome settlement."

He was outlining the parameters for marriage, one of life's deepest and most sacred commitments, as if it were a business deal in which every detail had to be pored over and ratified by attorneys. For all the emotion he was investing, they might as well have been discussing a shipment of bananas on its way to London in the hold of a Balfour freighter. Or going over construction change-orders for the St. Lucia resort Milo had told her his family was developing.

Her green eyes shot sparks. "You seem to have thought of everything, including the divorce," she jibed. "Don't tell me you overlooked custody provisions."

For a span of seconds, Ned saw what must have drawn Milo to her. Despite the washed-out look the gastric upsets of her pregnancy had given her, she had spirit, no mistake.

"As a matter of fact, I didn't," he answered imperturbably. "If we decide to split up at some future date, our child will attend boarding school here in England. His or her holidays will be equally divided between the two of us."

His casual tone made Jenny want to throttle him. He was talking about her baby as if he'd already acquired a stake in it. "Mr. Balfour," she said, digging her nails into her palms, "if you think for one minute..."

"If I were you, Miss McClain, I wouldn't make any snap judgments. Consider the alternatives. You've told me of your desire to make certain your child has the best in life, and I have no reason to doubt your sincerity. The arrangements I'm suggesting will accomplish that."

Offended as she was by the tenor of his proposal, she had to admit he had a point.

"You have a few days to think things over," he added, getting to his feet. "I leave for St. Lucia on the twenty-fifth. If we're to marry, we should do so before that date. Otherwise, your advancing pregnancy will make things a bit awkward, I should think."

Hugging herself in a plush corner of the Bentley as Ned Balfour's chauffeur drove her back to the Chelsea row house where she'd rented a room, Jenny shook her head. Incredibly, Ned wanted to give her baby his name—the very one it deserved by right of inheritance. The realization that, in the bargain, she could keep her child was similar to rising from a pit of despondency to find the brass ring on life's merry-go-round within her grasp.

To his credit, Ned had admitted his offer wasn't a selfless one. He'd also explained his reasons for making it. Yet she found it difficult to understand. With his money, drive and sex appeal, he'd have no problem attracting a mate and fathering a child of his own. What had happened to sour him so completely on love and trust?

She couldn't deny the benefits he was offering her were tremendous. By the single act of becoming his wife, she'd assure her child's future, and her own. Instead of aching over the gaping wound of their parting, she'd be on hand to witness her baby's first steps, shower it with good-night kisses. As she meditated on that miracle, her gratitude knew no bounds.

Yet he'd been wrong when he'd claimed the arrangements he was proposing involved little or no emotional risk. Despite the fact that she was expecting his brother's child and had given up on love, she couldn't ignore the dangerously unsettled feelings he evoked in her. Though they'd known each other just a few days, his touch, even his physical proximity profoundly affected her. She couldn't dismiss from her thoughts the memory of his dark eyes and broad shoulders.

Under the right circumstances, she guessed, she could have fallen in love with him. Instead she'd met Milo first and thoroughly disgraced herself. As a result, Ned would always despise her to a certain extent. At best, he viewed her as a charity case.

She could think of worse fates than marrying him. In his uncompromising way, he'd reminded her of them. Aside from the possibility of becoming attached to a man who had little respect for her and even less affection, she could see only a few major drawbacks to his proposal. The partial loss of her self-determination was one. Another centered on the fact that, henceforth, her primary residence wouldn't be in the United States.

Cynical as I've become, I don't like the notion of an arranged marriage, either, Jenny thought as Ned's chauffeur halted the Bentley at her doorstep. Apparently the incurable romantic in her, bloodied by her treatment at Milo's hands, wasn't totally bowed. She'd do well not to listen to it.

Letting herself in the row house's foyer with her key, she decided on impulse to phone her great-aunt. Though Jenny didn't plan to confide in her, with the possible exception of her missing father, Etta Nelson was her only living relative. Maybe she'd say something that would help Jenny make up her mind.

Dialing the overseas number at the spindly hall table where she'd taken Ned's call, she let the phone ring in her great-aunt's Ballard bungalow half a dozen times. At seventy-eight, Etta Nelson had severe osteoarthritis. Getting up from the lounger where she spent most of her time these days could be quite a task.

At last the older woman answered, her voice skeptical and aggressive despite her weakened condition and the vast geographical distance that separated them. "That you, Jennifer?" she asked in response to Jenny's determinedly cheery "Hello."

"Yes, Aunt Etta," Jenny replied, wondering if she'd made a mistake. "I thought I'd call and see how you were doing."

"Waste of money, child. Transatlantic phone connections aren't cheap. You coming home anytime soon?"

Jenny braced herself. "Perhaps not for a while," she admitted. "I might be getting married soon . . . to an Englishman."

Dead silence greeted the revelation. Then, "I hope he's not a bounder like your father," her great-aunt said disapprovingly. Something about her tone suggested anyone Jenny was apt to choose probably fit that category.

"He's a businessman, Aunt Etta," Jenny said defensively. "He has an excellent reputation."

The older woman's *"Hmmph"* expressed strong doubt. "If you want my advice, which you probably don't," she said, "get a ring on your finger before you jump into bed with him. Otherwise, you'll end up just like your mother did."

Ned was working late when the phone rang in his outer office. He's sent Liz Phipps home an hour earlier. Though it was probably a nuisance call, or some inconsequential matter his administrative assistant could handle in the morning, he decided to answer it.

"Ned Balfour here," he murmured, punching a button on his console.

"Mr. Balfour, it's Jennifer McClain." There was a slight pause, palpable with hesitation. "I've been thinking over your proposal," she added. "And, well . . . I've decided to accept."

For a moment, the line hummed, empty. Had he changed his mind? If the prospect of marriage without love or intimacy daunted him, she couldn't blame him.

That afternoon, as Ned had placed his brother's cast-off mistress in Ryerson's care, he'd guessed he had a twenty percent chance with her. They hadn't hit if off, at least not to his way of thinking. Yet at a deeper level, something had clicked. Whatever it was, he realized, neither of them felt very comfortable about it.

The important thing was that they both wanted her baby. Both were committed to fashioning the best possible life for it. Ned forced himself to control his irrational surge of excitement before answering her.

"Pardon me if I seem a bit taken aback," he said, his voice betraying only a hint of what he felt. "I didn't expect to hear from you so soon. Naturally I'm pleased with your decision. If it meets with your approval, we'll be married Monday or Tuesday. I'll get back to you in the morning with the details, after I've spoken to my solicitor."

Ryerson called for Jenny on Monday at 11:00 a.m. sharp. "Happy is the bride the sun shines on," she thought with a little twist of irony as she allowed the uniformed chauffeur to help her into the Bentley's back seat.

Yet if the weather was any sort of augury, surely her union with Ned Balfour would be blessed. Late the previous afternoon, the rain clouds that had hung over London for days had dispersed, leaving behind a blue vault of sky and balmy temperatures. In the trees, birds of every description were warbling. Flowers and light summery clothing seemed to be blossoming everywhere.

Despite the weather, Jenny had chosen a somber dress. One of the few that continued to fit her well, her navy linen shift had short sleeves and a plain, round neck. In an attempt to relieve its severity, she'd added a string of pearls.

As arranged, the chauffeur drove her first to the solicitor's office, which was situated in the Temple district. Ned was waiting by the curb, neatly groomed in a pin-striped suit. He'd tucked a carnation into his lapel.

"These are for you," he said, handing her a nosegay of gardenias as he helped her from the car.

She hadn't remotely expected such a gesture.

"Thanks... they're lovely," she whispered, keenly aware of the goose bumps that raced over her skin as his fingers brushed hers. "You needn't have troubled, though."

In response, the ghost of a smile played around his mouth. "I can't claim it was any bother. Mrs. Phipps ordered them."

His solicitor, Gerald Epping, who greeted them in a richly paneled office crammed with books, couldn't resist dropping his gaze momentarily to Jenny's stomach. He was plainly curious about the rushed character of their marriage. From several comments he made as they signed the papers he'd drawn up for them, Jenny got the strong impression he'd considered Ned a confirmed bachelor, unlikely to wed anyone. She felt a distinct shock, then, when he referred to her husband-to-be's first trip to the altar. The remark made her realize afresh how little she knew about the man she was marrying.

"I didn't know you'd been divorced," she said a few minutes later as she and Ned crossed a lush, green courtyard on their way to the magistrate's office.

Though something closed in his face, Ned didn't break his stride. "Why should you?" he asked with a shrug. "For your information, my wife, Veronica, and I went our separate ways four years ago. The problem was incompatibility. Since our own marriage is to be a more impersonal one, it shouldn't be a factor."

The magistrate Ned had engaged to perform the ceremony turned out to be a boyhood friend of his father. Peering at them through somewhat foggy spectacles, he shook their hands warmly after pronouncing them man and wife.

"Best of luck, old chap," he said. "You, too, Mrs. Balfour. Beat Milo and Pam to the altar, didn't you?"

In the caesura that followed, Ryerson tapped at the door. "Excuse me, sir," he addressed Ned with a worried expression. "But Mrs. Viv just reached me on the car phone. I'm sorry to say your grandfather's taken a turn for the worse. She and Mr. Oliver want you to drive down to Surrey immediately. They asked that you meet them at the Dorking hospital."

Chapter Three

In an instant, their itinerary had shifted. Instead of
going out to lunch and on to Ned's flat overlooking St.
Katherine's Dock, where the dust covers had been removed from the furniture and Jenny would reside with
a maid to care for her while he was in St. Lucia, they
headed south on the A-24 with Ryerson at the wheel.
As the Bentley ate up the miles, the man she'd married just a short time earlier seemed to have forgotten
her existence. His aspect brooding, he stared out the
window as urban sprawl blended into bedroom com-
munities and patches of woods.

Watching him, she didn't feel free to ask what kind
of reception they were likely to get. Or disturb his train
of thought by voicing her concern for him. She didn't
know him well and she'd never met his grandfather.
Whatever comfort she tried to offer might ring hol-
low in his ears. I hope we'll be returning to London
tonight, she thought, cut loose from every mooring

she knew and swept along by events. I don't even have a toothbrush.

Without anything but the scenery to distract her, she fell prey to the steady stream of questions that ran through her head. For instance, did Oliver and Viv Balfour, Ned's father and stepmother, have the slightest inkling he'd gotten married and would arrive with a pregnant bride in tow? Even more to the point, would they guess whose baby she was carrying?

Jenny was sure that, engaged as he was to the daughter of one of his father's wealthy business partners, Milo hadn't mentioned her to anyone. Yet for several weeks she and the younger Balfour son had spent a great deal of time in each other's company. It was entirely possible some neighbor or friend of the family had seen them together, and would recognize her.

She dreaded the prospect of coming face-to-face with Milo himself. *He* knew whose baby it was and, if he let the cat out of the bag, there'd be a family uproar. However he responded, she doubted if he'd be very pleased to see her. Though he'd insisted he didn't have the means to assist her financially, she had the distinct feeling he'd be angry with her for approaching Ned. One thing was certain. The moment he saw them together, he'd know that's what had taken place. There wasn't any other plausible way she and Ned could have met.

Charming and easygoing though he usually was, the Milo she knew wasn't above taunting her, or casting aspersions on his brother for coming to her rescue. If he wanted to, he could make things extremely unpleasant for them.

So far, everything Jenny had seen of the two men pointed to an underlying rift between them. During her brief relationship with him, Milo had expressed outright jealousy of Ned on several occasions. He'd seemed especially envious of his older brother's position of responsibility with the family firm. Though he hadn't appeared to care about Jenny and the child he'd fathered when he'd thought the problem they posed would resolve itself without his help, it was entirely possible he'd change his tune now that his take-charge sibling had entered the picture and proposed to raise the baby as his own.

I don't know what I expected to happen when I agreed to marry Ned, she groaned silently. I was thinking only of my little one. Yet all these complications are staring me in the face. She'd realized, of course, that she'd have to deal with Milo and meet the other Balfours eventually. But she'd never dreamed the necessity would arise within hours of the wedding ceremony.

The ancient market town of Dorking, situated on the North Downs south of Sandown Park racecourse, was just a short drive from London. It wasn't long before Ryerson was dropping them off at the hospital's main entrance and heading for the car park to wait for them.

At the reception desk, Ned learned his grandfather had been transferred to a private room. "I'll wait for you downstairs, if you'd like," Jenny offered hesitantly as they started for the lift.

Pausing in midstride, Ned gave her a focused look. In her navy shift and pearls, she looked fragile and extremely vulnerable. She clearly had strong reservations about meeting his family. Well, he couldn't blame her. Oliver, Viv and Margaret would jump to the conclusion that they'd had a love affair and gotten caught.

With his special knowledge of the situation, Milo could put an entirely different complexion on things. Ned didn't give a damn how his lazy, self-centered brother would feel about the unorthodox step he'd taken. In his view, Milo had abdicated his responsibility and he'd have to live with that. For the baby's sake, Ned planned to quash any attempt on Milo's part to trumpet the details of its parentage.

"C'mon," he said, encircling Jenny's shoulders with one arm as the lift door opened. "There'll be a few raised eyebrows. Together, we can handle them."

A graying strawberry blonde in her early fifties was carrying a foam cup filled with hot tea past the lift entrance when they emerged.

"Ned!" she exclaimed, nearly spilling its contents on his trousers as she gave him a hug. "Thank goodness you're here."

Cautiously he disengaged himself. "How's he doing, Viv?"

"Not very well."

A second later, the older woman had shifted her attention to Jenny. "Hello," she said. "I don't believe we know each other."

In what Jenny guessed must be his characteristic way of doing things, Ned met the situation head-on. "Viv, this is Jennifer McClain... Jennifer Balfour, as of this afternoon," he revealed. "We're expecting a baby in November. Jen, this is Vivian Chappell Balfour, my stepmother."

Shock drained the color from Viv's face, setting twin spots of blusher adrift in a sea of pasty white.

Jenny couldn't help flinching at the downward movement of her gaze.

"How do you do, Mrs. Balfour?" she said, striving to imitate Ned's nonchalance.

Viv's handshake was distinctly limp. "Pleased to make your acquaintance," she murmured. "American, aren't you? You'll have to pardon me, but this is something of a bombshell. Ned never said a word."

The man Jenny had married shrugged as if he was used to disconcerting people. "Jennifer and I have been dating for some time," he assured his stepmother blandly. "I was afraid she wouldn't marry me if she met the family first. American distrust of wealthy Brits or some such rubbish, I believe."

Obviously more shocked than ever, Viv glanced at Jenny for denial or confirmation.

"You know how Ned is," the latter improvised, implying a familiarity with her new husband she didn't possess. "He tends to exaggerate."

His gaze applauded her. A moment later, he'd returned it to Viv. "What do you say we go in and see Grandfather?" he suggested.

In the no-frills room crammed with state-of-the-art medical equipment, Jenny's eyes were drawn first to the gaunt, white-haired man who lay motionless in his hospital bed. An oxygen cannula had been inserted in his nose. Wires and tubes connected him to a heart monitor and a metal IV stand hung with multiple bags of clear fluid. Though he was old and sick, his family resemblance to the man she'd married was striking. They appeared to have been cut from the same cloth.

"Grandfather, it's Ned," the latter whispered, gently stroking the old man's hand.

His words didn't evoke a flicker of response. Glancing up, Jenny saw Viv whisper something into the ear of a balding, stylish man in tweeds she guessed was Ned's father. He stared at her in blank surprise. Apparently the news about their marriage and her condition wouldn't take long to circulate. Thanks to Ned's flip revelation of her pregnancy and flimsy excuse for keeping his family in the dark about their plans, his father and stepmother had probably formed an unfavorable impression of her.

To her relief, Milo was nowhere around. The only other person in the room was a brown-haired woman in her mid-thirties Jenny concluded must be Ned and Milo's sister, Margaret. She learned her guess was correct a moment later when Ned introduced them. Though they were polite, even welcoming to a point, it wasn't difficult to see that, like Viv, Oliver and Margaret Balfour were dumfounded Ned should have married her.

They didn't stay long after that. When a nurse appeared to complain about the number of family members crowded into the tiny room, Ned volunteered to leave and come back later. He nodded at Jenny. "My wife needs a chance to rest. And something to eat."

In contrast to the A-24, their drive to Longwood, the Balfour country estate situated between the villages of Friday Street and Holmsbury St. Mary, took them along winding roads sunk deep in the underlying sandstone beneath overarching trees. At last they turned in at a private, unmarked lane flanked by boxwood and massive oaks. At its end, a mellow red brick house with matching wings shone like a jewel at the center of its woodland park. Its design was pure eighteenth century. A two-story recessed portico in the Palladian style and broad stone steps bid them a muted, refined welcome.

"It's wonderful, Ned," Jenny said, unconsciously addressing him for the first time by his given name.

He threw her an appraising glance. "I'm fond of it."

There were no bags to unload and, once Ned had helped her from the car, Ryerson proceeded in the direction of the garage. As they started up the steps, an elderly butler opened the door.

"Welcome home, Mr. Ned. Good day, miss," he said with a dignified smile, admitting them and taking their raincoats. "Everyone's at the hospital but Mr. Milo. I believe he's in the den."

Oh, no, Jenny thought in dismay. I'm not ready for this.

Ned took her firmly by the arm. "Maxwell," he said, "this is my wife, Jennifer. We got married this afternoon. Please ask Mrs. Burke to fix us tea and sandwiches while we say hello to my brother."

Leaving the astonished butler to stare after them, he propelled her across the black-and-white marble checkerboard of the spacious foyer toward the west wing.

"If you don't mind, I'd rather you talked to Milo alone," she protested faintly.

Ned's dark brows knitted together in a frown. "What are you afraid of?"

"I'm not anxious to see him. If he tells the rest of your family about us . . ."

"I won't permit it."

Seconds later, he was throwing open the study door. Light haired and handsome in tweeds and country cords, Milo was leaning against the room's elegant mantel, brandy snifter in hand. Glancing in their direction, he looked from Ned to Jenny and back again. "What is this?" he asked, appearing to take their presence as a de facto indictment. "The morality police, come to make me honor my obligations?"

Jenny flinched. The brandy Milo was holding clearly hadn't been his first. She doubted the coming scene would be a pleasant one.

On the surface, at least, Ned let his brother's sarcastic comment roll off his back. "I don't know what you're talking about," he answered, advancing into the room. "Nobody's asking you to do anything. Since you already know my wife, Jennifer, I won't bother to introduce you. I thought you might want to wish us well."

"Jenny's... *your wife?*"

The wind knocked briefly from his sails, Milo absorbed the news. "Well, I'll be damned," he said slowly, as if pleased at the chance to savage his brother. "You really do have a penchant for damaged goods."

The transformation in Ned was instantaneous. Jenny let out a gasp of disbelief as his fist connected with Milo's jaw. Caught off guard, the man who'd fathered Jenny's baby reeled backward, knocking over a lamp with a resounding crash. Simultaneously his brandy glass smashed against the grate, flooding the room with the scent of alcohol.

"I know you're drunk, but try to show a little respect," Ned growled, noting Jenny's sharply indrawn breath and misinterpreting the reason for it. "My wife's going to wonder what kind of family this is."

"By God, that's rich." Dabbing with his pocket handkerchief at a thin trickle of blood that had appeared at one corner of his mouth, Milo got to his feet. "You do know she's pregnant?" he asked, flicking a shard of expensive, hand-painted porcelain from his sleeve. "And who the father is?"

Ned didn't regret punching Milo in the mouth, but he had no intention of inflicting serious injury. There was such a thing as family. "When Jennifer's baby is born," he replied evenly, "*I'll* be the father. If you have a problem with that, I suggest we settle it now... right here, in this room."

Drunk as he was, Milo couldn't hide a flicker of uncertainty. Despite his three-inch advantage in height, it was obvious he couldn't match Ned's physical strength or hard but supple conditioning. In a fight that pitted them against each other, he was sure to get the worst of it.

"I don't imagine Father will thank us for trashing another of his lamps," he answered, summoning a cocky grin. "As for Jenny, if you want her, she's yours. I have no interest in her. Or the brat she's carrying."

Drunk or not, Jenny burned to slap his good-looking face. She clenched her fists in frustration.

Ned grasped Milo by the lapels. "I warned you to show some manners," he said, his face a stern vision just inches from his brother's. "If you use the term 'brat' again in reference to my heir *or* tell tales out of school, I'll make you the sorriest..."

The doubts he cast on Milo's legitimacy made Jenny blush. When it came to making good on his word, she felt certain Ned was fully capable.

Apparently the duel of words and growing discomfort in his jaw were beginning to have a sobering effect on Milo. "How do you plan to stop me?" he asked in a blatant attempt to regain his self-respect. "By beating me to a pulp like some schoolyard bully?"

"If I bloody well feel like it, I will," Ned said. "But I doubt it'll be necessary. As CEO of Balfour Shipping, I have the power of the checkbook."

Though the outward shell of Milo's manner remained defiant, it was clear Ned had scored a hit. Milo needed the allowance his older brother dispensed every month to cover his gambling debts and maintain his profligate life-style.

Just then, footsteps echoed on the hall's marble tiles. They were about to have an audience.

A moment later, Viv poked her head in the door. "What on earth's going on in here?" she demanded. "My God...the lamp...there's glass all over the place!"

Ned declined to answer. Behind Viv, Oliver Balfour was surveying the damage to his study with narrowed eyes. It would be up to Milo to explain, Jenny realized.

Straightening his jacket, the playboy who'd sunk to a new low in Jenny's estimation struck a jaunty pose. "Same old sibling rivalry, Dad," he joked.

It was a feeble attempt at humor, and Oliver clearly wasn't amused. However, he didn't seem inclined to pursue the issue with his father so ill. "I suggest you sober up and have Maxwell dispose of this mess," he told his younger son, fixing him with a steely gaze. "Come on, Viv. After hanging about the hospital all afternoon, I could use a nap."

Without another word to Milo, Ned took Jenny by
the hand and followed them upstairs. The tea and
sandwiches he'd ordered had been arranged on a low
table in the sitting area of his rust, tan-and-navy-blue
bedroom.

Still burning over her embarrassing introduction to
the rest of the Balfours, Jenny felt as if she ought to
apologize. Because of her, she believed, the family was
in an uproar as its oldest member lay sick and in danger.

Perhaps guessing what she had in mind, Ned fore-
stalled any confession of guilt. "What happened
downstairs is a closed chapter," he told her in no uncertain terms. "When he sobers up, Milo will realize
that and comply with my wishes."

Not answering, she looked around the room. In
addition to the grouping of love seat and easy chairs,
a four-poster bed, dresser and heavy, masculine-
looking armoire, it contained a desk and a computer-
printer Ned probably used to access his data bank at
the office. The artwork was impersonal—a collection
of hunt-country serigraphs Viv had doubtless chosen
to harmonize with the decorating scheme. There were
no knickknacks or family photos.

If his boudoir was any indication, Ned *was* all business, as his less-than-admiring brother had claimed.
Yet Jenny sensed there was another side to him. He
might be controlled and pragmatic, but he seemed
genuinely fond of his grandfather. He'd been passionate enough to attack his brother for insulting her.
He seemed to care how she felt.

"Though you probably don't feel like it, for the
baby's sake you ought to eat something," he advised,
waving her to the tan-and-navy-striped sateen love

seat. "Dinner will be at eight. You'll have plenty of time for a nap first. If you like, you may borrow one of my robes."

Chances are we'll be expected to sleep together if we stay over, Jenny thought. Most couples do on their wedding night. Yet he'd promised her intimacy wouldn't be an issue.

"What do you plan to do this afternoon?" she asked.

His answer didn't shed any light on what she could expect later. "My grandfather's in pretty bad shape," he answered. "I thought I'd go back to the hospital and sit with him for a while."

By the time Ned returned, it was nearly half past seven. The tea things had been removed and Jenny was fast asleep beneath his goose-down comforter. It felt odd yet somehow reassuring to find her there, nestled in his bastion of male solitude.

About to wake her, he stayed his hand. Curled on her side, with her surprisingly long lashes as dark as soot against cheeks that had flushed rose-colored from the comforter's warmth, she seemed more child than woman. It was hard to believe she was expecting a baby—one he would call his own.

As yet, they were strangers. Relaxing his mental prohibitions against it, Ned let himself imagine what it would be like to have a personal relationship with her. She was obviously intelligent. And not bad-looking. When their eyes had met in the mirrors aboard his yacht, hers had revealed a sensual interest that stunned him with its intensity.

If they became lovers someday, despite his vow to keep their union on a strictly platonic footing...

Pushing the thought from him, Ned pictured her in Milo's arms. No doubt she'd gazed at his brother and the wealth she'd thought he had at his disposal with sensual interest, too. That's all you need, he thought in disgust—to get emotionally involved with Milo's cast-off mistress, no matter how appealing and innocent she might seem. A moment later, he conceded her feelings for his brother might have been genuine. It had been all too easy to speculate, from the way she'd behaved during their confrontation in the study, that she was still in love with him.

If their marriage-in-name-only was to function as he hoped, they'd both have to abide by the rules. Resolved to play his part, Ned roused her with a light touch. "Dinner in half an hour," he said casually. "If you like, you may use the bathroom first."

Washing her face and combing her hair, Jenny donned her navy shift. While it was creased and lacking in style, it was more appropriate than Ned's bathrobe—her only alternative choice. She hoped the rest of the Balfours wouldn't turn up at the table in formal attire.

Perhaps in deference to her, they didn't. Despite the family cook's best efforts and Viv's determined attempts to get a conversation going, dinner was an ordeal. Oliver and Ned were plainly worried. In addition to Andrew Balfour's illness, the awkwardness of Ned's precipitous marriage and his impending fatherhood weighted the table talk like a stone. Picking at her food, Jenny was grateful that at least Milo hadn't seen fit to join them. If Ned's grandfather was stable enough, she hoped they could return to the city for the night.

She was not to get her wish. They'd just arisen when Maxwell summoned Oliver to the phone. He returned a minute or two later, his expression grim.

"Father's had another stroke," he said, addressing Viv as he popped a nitroglycerin tablet for his heart. "We'd better get back to the hospital."

"I'll go with you," Ned offered at once.

Noting that the number of visitors the family patriarch could have at one time was limited, Margaret elected not to make the trip. Jenny promptly pleaded a headache. Undressing partway in the privacy of her husband's room, she crawled between the sheets and switched off the lamp.

Keenly aware of her unfamiliar surroundings, she found it difficult to sleep. Around 1:00 a.m., she heard a car drive up. Getting out of bed and going over to the window, she saw Viv and Oliver emerge from the Bentley and mount the front steps. It was impossible to tell whether Ned or Ryerson was at the wheel. A moment later, the big, black car headed up the driveway, presumably on its way back to the hospital.

It was dawn. Stirring at the slight sound Ned made as he tossed his billfold and keys onto the dresser, Jenny opened her eyes. It was obvious he hadn't slept. A stubble of beard darkened his jaw, making him look both tough and sorrowful. Weariness was etched in his every line and aspect.

"Ned?" she murmured.

"Go back to sleep."

"How's your grandfather? Is he doing any better?"

"He died an hour ago."

"Oh, *no*. I'm so sorry! Is there anything I can do?"

Turning back the covers without regard for the fact that she'd slept in her laciest, most revealing slip, Jenny got up and padded over to him. "Please . . . stretch out and get some rest," she urged. "I've had more than enough. If you're hungry, I can sneak down to the kitchen and fix you something."

None of the Balfour women had cooked for their men in recent memory. Touched despite his reservations about her, Ned shook his head. "Thanks, I don't think I could eat just now. Why don't you get back under the covers? I'll be out of here in a minute or so."

As oblivious to the conventions as she because of the loss he'd just suffered, he stripped to his shorts. While Jenny watched, he stepped into corduroy trousers, zipping them up and pulling a heather-gray woolen sweater over his head.

"Where are you going?" she asked.

"Leith Hill. I need to regain my perspective."

"Let me come with you."

About to refuse, Ned hesitated. He wasn't at all sure he wanted company. It was just that he felt so damnably alone. "All right," he agreed. "Put on some clothes."

Dressed in her by-now-despised navy shift, with one of Ned's cardigan sweaters buttoned over it and a silk square she carried in her purse knotted beneath her chin, Jenny accompanied him downstairs. The rest of the household continued to slumber. Settling her in the Bentley's front passenger seat, Ned got in behind the wheel.

At that hour, Leith Hill, a well-known promontory and picnic spot within easy driving distance of Longwood via the Abinger road, was deserted. Its observation tower, dating from the eighteenth century, was locked and bolted. Yet, even at ground level, the view was spectacular. Catching fire with the rising sun as it burned the diamond incrustation of dew from the grass, a sweeping panorama of farmland and woods spread out before them.

For what seemed eons, Jenny stood at Ned's side, offering her wordless presence.

"A life for a life," he muttered at last, squinting against the sun's brilliance.

"You mean . . ."

"My grandfather's gone. But we'll have your baby."

They got back into the car. About to turn his key in the ignition, Ned paused to rest one arm on the steering wheel and lean his head against it. Abruptly the tears he'd fought back at the hospital had started to flow.

"Ned," Jenny whispered in anguish, not knowing how to comfort him.

His reply was fierce. "I miss him already, damn it."

"Come here," she said. "Let me hold you."

With a barely audible groan, he turned and buried his face against her neck.

Chapter Four

They buried Ned's grandfather three days later in the Balfour family plot beside a private eighteenth-century chapel on the estate grounds. It was a balmy spring day. Birds were warbling in the trees. As if to mock the grief of the friends and family members who'd gathered to bid him farewell, the sky was innocent of clouds.

Throughout the service, Jenny could feel Milo staring at her. He probably wasn't the only one. If the covert glances and whispers that had greeted their arrival were any indication, her sudden marriage to Ned and impending motherhood had created quite a stir.

Grateful for the smart black trapeze dress Viv had ordered sent down from a London shop and resolved not to flinch no matter how fierce the scrutiny became, she concentrated on Ned. He was standing next to her and she couldn't help wincing at the muscle that contracted in his jaw when the casket was lowered into the ground. His fists clenched as Oliver threw the first handful of dirt on its lid.

Though his eyes were suspiciously damp when it was his turn, he didn't weep. Milo was next, then Margaret, then Jenny. Never having known Andrew Balfour and uneasy about her inclusion in the family circle, Jenny stepped forward to release her contribution of crumbled earth.

A moment later she was tensing at her new brother-in-law's sarcastic whisper.

"Made a proper spectacle of yourself, haven't you?" he said. "They'll never accept you...not in a million years."

She didn't give him the satisfaction of a reply.

Watching them together, Ned felt a stab of something akin to jealousy in his gut. He tried to tell himself it was misplaced. He wasn't emotionally involved with Jenny. And she'd done nothing that would remotely violate her pledge not to shame him with his brother. Whatever her feelings for Milo, in the days leading up to the funeral she'd made a point of avoiding him.

Unfortunately Jenny's connection to the sibling who'd helped his ex-wife cheat on him was impossible to forget. By the age of thirty-nine, Ned had been married to two women. And the brother he disliked so intensely had bedded them both.

He couldn't help mentioning the incident when he and Jenny got into the Bentley to return to the house. "I saw Milo speak to you at the graveside," he observed, keeping his voice expressionless. "Did he say anything I should know about?"

The last thing Jenny wanted was to repeat Milo's hurtful taunt. She already felt thoroughly out of place.

Yet she couldn't allow Ned to think his brother was trying to revive their affair.

"I can't recall his exact words," she prevaricated. "In general, their purpose was to humiliate me."

Though he was relieved in one sense, Ned's nerves were still raw from the burial. "I warned him I wouldn't tolerate that sort of thing," he scowled.

Jenny cringed at his tone. Too easily, she could imagine what might take place. As before, Ned and Milo would argue. Ned would punch him in the mouth. This time, a houseful of guests and mourners would witness it.

She dared to rest one hand on his sleeve. "Ned, *please* ..."

His eyes stony with displeasure, he waited.

"Out of respect for your grandfather's memory, shouldn't we try to keep the peace this afternoon?"

Anger warred with his sense of propriety and lost. "You're right, of course," he conceded. "I'll do my best to be civilized."

They left for London early the next morning, while Milo was still abed. As the Bentley slid into rush-hour traffic, Ned's mask of confident control was firmly back in place. Jenny could scarcely believe he'd allowed Milo to ruffle his composure at the funeral. Or, on the morning of his grandfather's death, let down his guard with her.

Following a brief stop at his office to pick up a set of construction plans and other documents, they retrieved Jenny's meager possessions from her bed-sitting room and installed them in his flat at St. Katherine Dock, where Ryerson and a housekeeper would look after her while Ned was out of the country.

The place was spacious and well-appointed though she couldn't discern a particular decorating style. Sunlight poured in through the living-room windows, splashing on parquet floors strewn with faded Oriental rugs and leather furniture. His bookcases overflowed with books.

Moving her in didn't take long. When they'd finished, Ned was seized with a fit of restlessness. He'd had to postpone his St. Lucia trip twice—once to marry Jenny and once because of his grandfather's death. Now he wanted to get it over with. To that effect, he'd phoned British Airways before leaving Longwood to request the earliest available departure date.

To his chagrin, the flight he wanted was fully booked for a week. Determined to get the family resort project under way now that he'd cleared the decks for that purpose and attracted by the prospect of putting some distance between himself and recent events, he'd asked the ticket agent to jot down his London number in case of a cancellation.

Now he was pacing and talking of going back to the office. Though she said nothing, Jenny hoped he wouldn't be able to leave right away. In less time than she'd have thought possible, he'd gone from adversary to lifeline. Her heart sank when the agent called back around 4:00 p.m. to say a seat had opened up. If Mr. Balfour could leave for Heathrow at once . . .

He could, indeed. His bags were already packed.

"You needn't bother to see me off," he murmured as Ryerson collected his cases and carried them downstairs. "It's just a business trip. While I'm away, I trust you'll follow a sensible routine and get plenty of rest."

He'd be gone two months.

Take me with you, she longed to plead as he adjusted his cuff links and gave her a swift, perfunctory hug. But she didn't dare. She'd agreed his private life would be his own. Maybe he had a girlfriend on St. Lucia. The notion bothered her all out of proportion to her stake in him.

"Take care of yourself, too," she answered, forbidding her lower lip to tremble. "And please don't worry. With Ryerson and Mrs. Finch watching over us, the baby and I will be all right."

With little to do in Ned's absence but shop for a layette and choose a few maternity outfits for herself, Jenny had ample time to settle in and explore. She quickly found that, unlike his room at Longwood and the trim, shipshape cabin on his sailing yacht, Ned's flat was brimming with clues to his personality and taste.

Among his books were volumes on astronomy and contemporary British art, complemented by the gleaming, tripod-mounted telescope that stood in front of his living-room windows and the original watercolors and oils scattered around the apartment. His compact disc collection ranged from Bach and Delius to Paul Simon, the Beatles and Miles Davis.

An armoire was crammed with sporting equipment. On his computer desk beneath a framed collection of antique political cartoons, a pair of horn-rimmed reading glasses lay forgotten atop a sheaf of papers. For some reason, the farsightedness they revealed made her think of the vulnerability that had surprised her so much. Neatly arranged on their wooden hangers, the suits he'd left behind in his London closet carried his elusive scent.

Without question, Ned Balfour was a complex man. One obsessed with business, as Milo had said, yet an art and music lover. An exercise fanatic, he liked to read and observe the heavens. She hadn't failed to note that he exuded sex appeal from every pore.

He was also her husband, though not in the usual sense. As she lay in bed at night, her head resting on the smooth percale cases that adorned his guest-room pillows, Jenny tried to pin down the tangle of emotions she felt.

At first she hadn't liked him much. He'd asked such blatant questions, making her feel like a scared rabbit and a scarlet woman, almost in the same breath. Now that she knew him a little better, she was drawn to him despite herself. His enigmatic comment that he, too, had lost at love caused her endless speculation.

Near the beginning of her fourth month, Jenny's baby moved. She was standing before a display of red bell peppers, avocados and shiny purple eggplants at Spitalfields Market when it happened—a tremulous flutter that could easily have been mistaken for indigestion.

Going absolutely still, she rested one hand on the slight swell of her abdomen. A moment later, the slight stirring reasserted itself. This time there wasn't any doubt about its source. Tears of happiness that she and the precious child she carried would know each other and bond in love pushed against her eyelids.

"Are you all right, miss?" the portly vendor asked.

She gave him a beatific smile. "Oh, *yes*..."

Ryerson, who'd driven her from the flat and followed her from stall to stall in case he was needed to
carry something had approached her, too.

"Do you want me to get the car, madam?" he said
with a worried look.

What I want, Jenny thought with a wave of longing, is for Ned to be here beside me. At the very least
for him to come home tonight and kick back in his
favorite chair so I can tell him what took place.
Though he didn't love her and he wasn't her child's
father in a physical sense, the man she'd married so
precipitously had assumed the latter position in her
head.

He wouldn't be back for at least a month. And she
didn't have anyone else to share her wonder with.

Reminding herself how lucky she was, just to have
his name and support, she turned her glowing face to
the chauffeur. "Not yet, Ryerson," she answered
gently. "There's nothing to be concerned about."

Jenny's baby didn't make its presence felt again for
the rest of the day. That evening, after Ryerson and
Mrs. Finch had bid her good-night and gone down to
their efficiency flats on the floor below, loneliness descended over her like a pall. Gathering her courage,
she sat down at her husband's desk.

"Dear Ned," her letter began. "The most commonplace yet miraculous thing happened this morning—the baby moved! I was shopping for produce and
suddenly there it was, this faint fluttering, as if he or
she were stretching, trying out the use of a tiny hand
or foot. I felt something close to awe shiver down my
arms. A feeling of gratitude and love and commitment wrapped itself around me like a coat."

I wish you could have been there to share it....

Pausing, Jenny arrested her pen in its trajectory across the sheet of cream-colored stationery she'd withdrawn from the middle drawer of Ned's desk. Abruptly the words she'd been about to commit to paper embarrassed her. He's going to think you're crazy, she told herself. Not to mention presumptuous. You don't have that kind of relationship with him.

Moments later, the letter that had flowed from her heart lay crumpled in the wastebasket. Taking a fresh sheet, she described the event that had so moved her in more matter-of-fact terms. As the wife in name only that she was, she added her best wishes for the success of his project and the assurance that she was doing well.

As Jenny was to learn, letters sent via the regular post took their time to travel between London and St. Lucia. And like her, Ned chose not to phone. Nearly a month elapsed before she had his reply in hand. By then she was almost five months along and her baby was moving regularly. She tore open the envelope with trembling fingers.

A half-dozen snapshots tumbled out. One featured a view of Castries harbor from the bluff above the resort. Two showed a pink stucco hotel and construction in progress with a palm-lined cove and the Caribbean in the background.

The others he'd sent depicted an aging, two-story brick house with porches on three sides, the island's vertiginous twin peaks, known as Pitons, and a shuttered, drunken-looking cottage on stilts painted a bright orchid color. The cottage was hip-deep in coconut palms and ragged, tender banana leaves. In its yard, a clothesline billowed with vivid garments.

It had been a gray and rainy summer in London. To Jenny, St. Lucia's extravagant greenery and brilliant sunlight looked like an earthly paradise.

Ned's accompanying note was brief, dashed off in the showy, barely legible scrawl with which he'd signed the marriage register. In it, he urged her to take care of herself and her child. He also mentioned that, because of problems he'd encountered with both materials and labor, he probably wouldn't return to London before the first of September.

That's three months from now, Jenny thought in dismay. Meanwhile, my life is like a vacuum. I'm not sure I can bear the solitude.

On impulse, she asked Ryerson to drive her to the nearest telegraph office, where she wired her husband with a daring message: *I've never seen the Caribbean. And I'm lonely here. Would you mind if I joined you?*

Once her telegram was sent, she had second thoughts. Ned had stressed noninterference in each other's lives when they'd discussed the terms of their marriage. Again the possibility that he had a romance going on in St. Lucia raised its head.

If he did, she knew, he wouldn't want a pregnant wife underfoot. Yet she couldn't keep from hoping he wouldn't object to having her around. When his answer came, it was succinct and typical of the man: *Come if you want.*

The following day, Ned's assistant, Nigel Carstairs, called to say his boss had asked him to arrange her trip. On his advice, Jenny traveled on a jumbo jet to Barbados and transferred to a smaller plane for the short hop to Vigie Airport near Castries.

Hewanorra Airport, the larger St. Lucian facility that served transatlantic flights, was situated an hour's drive from Castries near the island's southern tip. Famous though it was for its banana plantations and dramatic views of waves crashing against the tiny nation's rugged east coast, the road that connected Hewanorra with her destination was a dusty horror of hairpin turns and potholes, Nigel had told her. His implication had been clear. An expectant mother would be wise to avoid the jarring it entailed.

Her face pressed to the glass, Jenny watched St. Lucia's west coast come into view. She saw lush green hills, beaches like brown sugar. As they flew over Castries Harbor and came in for a landing, they passed a bluff studded with private homes and what might have been tin-roofed army barracks built during a previous century. Its green hump was ablaze with the red-orange blossoms of flamboyant trees.

In just minutes, she'd be face-to-face with Ned. His assistant had mentioned that he planned to meet her plane. Keenly aware of the changes her advancing pregnancy had wrought and wondering how he'd react to them, Jenny applied fresh lipstick and patted her hair in place.

Ned was waiting on the runway outside the customs shed as she disembarked. Though she recognized him at once, it struck her that, superficially at least, his island self was a separate incarnation from the man she'd met.

For the first time in her memory of him, he appeared completely relaxed. His hair was rumpled, his skin bronzed from a surfeit of outdoor activity. Instead of a business suit, he wore khaki shorts and an open-necked cotton shirt. Its short sleeves rippled against his upper arms in the lively breeze off the nearby harbor.

Ned shaded his eyes against the sun as he looked Jenny over from head to foot. He couldn't hide his interest as his gaze lingered on her abdomen for several seconds before he returned it to her face.

Can this be the bedraggled, emotionally drowning young woman who walked into my office in May? he asked himself. The Jenny he'd known had been a pallid, sickly ghost compared with the radiant mother-to-be who negotiated the portable metal steps while keeping her eyes fixed on him.

For her trip, she'd chosen a white-linen shift that left her slender arms bare and skimmed the burgeoning shape of her unborn child. Her breasts were rounder, more luxurious. They reminded him of ripening fruit. Begun in discomfort and unhappiness, her pregnancy agreed with her. Roses had bloomed in her cheeks.

"Hello, Jen," he said in his gruff voice, extending his hand as he came forward to greet her.

"Hi," she answered.

His palm was calloused, his fingers warm and strong as they gripped hers. A little stab of some undefined emotion passed through her. In vain she tried to read what he was thinking. Hidden behind dark glasses, his eyes didn't offer a clue.

"How was your flight?" he asked after a moment.

"Good." He was still holding her hand. She wondered if he realized it. "Nigel sent me first class," she elaborated. "My seat was so comfortable, I slept."

Imagining her soft, even breathing as she nestled against a regulation airline pillow and dreamed the dreams of an expectant mother high above the Atlantic, Ned thought of the letter he'd received the day before. Viv had written to tell him of Milo's ruptured engagement. Apparently his brother and Pam Fitz-herbert had called it off at Pam's request.

According to Ned's stepmother, Milo's intended had developed a crush on her riding instructor. I wonder if the breakup had anything to do with Jenny's eagerness to leave London, Ned speculated. It's possible that, with Milo free, she doesn't trust herself. If so, at least she was doing her best to keep her bargain with him.

Aware of the question in his eyes, Jenny had no idea what it was. Pausing to collect her luggage, he escorted her through customs. The smiling official who questioned her in musical, hard-to-understand English turned out to be the brother of Ned's construction foreman, and the formalities didn't take long. Before she'd had time to adjust to the fact that she was really *there,* in St. Lucia with him, Ned had stowed her bags into a brown-and-tan Jeep, from which he'd removed the canvas top, and helped her into its passenger seat.

On St. Lucia, it seemed, he drove himself. Turning his key in the Jeep's ignition, he shifted gears. Like the British, to whose Commonwealth they'd recently belonged, St. Lucians drove on the left. They took off in a burst of speed, circling the end of the runway and merging into the main road that led to town. Immediately the breeze stirred up by their passage caught at Jenny's hair, loosening it from its demure Edwardian knot.

Traffic intensified as they passed the modern, duty-free shopping complex Ned said was called Pointe Seraphine. He was forced to slow the jeep's progress. Jenny noted a great many multipassenger vans emblazoned with the logos of touring companies.

Inadvertently she found herself gazing at the play of muscles in Ned's thigh as he transferred his foot from brake to gas pedal. He was every bit as compact, as beautifully made as she remembered. A moment later she was concentrating on the scenery and blushing at what she considered to be her own concupiscence.

Despite the stop-and-go traffic, they were soon immersed in the teeming, inelegant city of Castries. Horns honked. People jaywalked with little apparent regard for life and limb. It was Saturday and a throng of local vendors had set up shop on the sidewalks surrounding the bustling covered market. Cheap jewelry, craft items and every conceivable variety of tropical vegetable and fruit were spread out on tableclothes and blankets. The hive of commercial activity spilled into the street.

Though the atmosphere was one of poverty, the air fairly rang with good cheer and the cries of entrepreneurship. Accustomed to Seattle and more recently acquainted with the sophistication and glamour of London, Jenny stared. She realized with a jolt that St. Lucia must be what was known as a third-world country. She was very far from home.

Watching her, Ned hadn't forgotten his reservations about the purpose of her visit. But he couldn't help smiling a little at what he guessed were her mingled curiosity and feelings of disorientation as she drank in the unfamiliar sights.

To be honest, he hadn't thought much about her and the baby she carried during their time apart. Instead he'd tried to focus on the job at hand. Now he was experiencing a culture shock of sorts himself. Continuing to glance at her as he negotiated Castries' narrow streets and drove past the working port where

Balfour Shipping's freighters docked, he felt a strong sense of possessiveness toward the child that distended her belly. The infant he'd agreed to raise as his son or daughter had suddenly become a real person to him.

He was mesmerized, too, by the surprising fact that, in her simple white maternity dress, the forlorn, discarded woman to whom he'd offered his name and protection was actually quite beautiful. It was all he could do to keep from reaching out to touch her cheek. Her mouth is like crushed strawberries, he thought distractedly. If I'd known she could glow like that, I might not have married her.

The resort property, which Ned said encompassed a former estate, private golf course and existing hotel, ran along a coconut-fringed creek between a cove washed by the sea and a steep, forested bluff that rose to become part of Morne Fortune, the elongated, flat-topped mountain that overlooked the city and its harbor.

By the time the Balfours had finished, he told her, it would boast tiered bungalows, attached cottages and an open-air restaurant grouped around the hotel, which was currently in the process of renovation. There'd be tennis courts, an area set aside for water sports, two swimming pools.

Giving her a quick tour of the grounds, he pointed out the various endeavors that had claimed his attention since his arrival from England. Though the work appeared to be very different from that which usually occupied him, Jenny sensed he'd been enjoying himself. As they talked, breakers crashed on the smooth, tan beach, their boom and hiss blending with the sound of the Jeep and the hammering of construction.

At last Ned threw the Jeep's engine into second gear for their ascent up a steep grade to the two-story brick house Jenny remembered from one of the photographs he's sent.

"This is it," he said, tossing her a look as they pulled into a gravel parking space. "My humble abode. I trust you'll be comfortable here. I've arranged an appointment for you with a local obstetrician in the morning so that, healthwise you'll be on solid ground."

Considering the prospect of getting used to a new doctor, Jenny gazed at the house. Though it looked as if it could use a little sprucing up here and there, it was anything but modest. Constructed of the same weathered tan brick as the former military barracks she'd seen just before landing and topped by a corrugated tin roof that had oxidized to a rusty red, it had a commanding view of the resort, the city and the harbor.

Flame-colored bougainvillea and another flowering vine she didn't recognize clambered up the wrought-iron columns of its wraparound porch, shading an old-fashioned rattan swing, wooden rockers, an informal dining table. Tall louvered shutters framed its floor-to-ceiling windows.

Thrusting his keys into his pocket, Ned helped Jenny from the Jeep. They were greeted in a lilting patois that sounded as if it contained elements of English, French and African dialects by one of the Balfour gardeners, who unloaded Jenny's bags.

Inside, the house was open, airy and sparsely furnished with antiques. Arabella, a slender young woman Ned introduced as his temporary housekeeper, shook hands with Jenny and beckoned them to lunch on the porch.

The fresh lobster salad with curry and fruit that awaited them was one of the most spectacular dishes Jenny had ever tasted. She tackled it with gusto, in part to avoid Ned's enigmatic regard. But though she gave it her best effort, she was too excited and worn-out to eat very much.

"Time for me to get back to work and you to take a nap," Ned announced when she put down her fork.

I don't *want* to sleep, Jenny thought. Now that I'm here, I want to savor every moment. Yet she had to admit he was right. Her baby's welfare had to come first. Unaccountably the longing she'd felt in Spital-fields Market when her child had moved for the first time returned full force.

Seldom heeded, the risk-taker in her soul was ad-vocating something Ned might find presumptuous. "All right," she agreed hesitantly, wondering if she had the gumption to do as she wished. "I'll lie down for a while if you'll walk me upstairs."

Arabella could just as easily show her to her room, Ned thought. Concealing his sudden impatience to be gone so he could regain something of his bachelor perspective, he did as she asked. He was speechless when, as they entered what would be her private re-treat, she took his hand and placed it on the curve of her stomach.

Almost immediately, the light pressure brought a fluttering response. Ned's pupils widened. It was the baby, moving beneath his palm.

Jenny's mouth relaxed at the awe he couldn't hide. "*This* is what I've wanted to show you since I wrote you that first letter," she confessed, trusting a bit more

readily to her instincts. "It seemed the perfect opportunity. He's been kicking me unmercifully since I got
off the plane."

The baby moved again and Ned was transfixed by
the profound intimacy of an experience he'd never
hoped to share. "What makes you think it's a boy?"
he asked unsteadily.

"I just do."

They gazed silently at each other.

"What would you say to naming him Andrew, after your grandfather?" she suggested after a moment.

While Jenny napped between breeze-scented sheets,
Ned tried to concentrate on his work. Totally immersed in it before her arrival, he couldn't seem to
keep his mind from wandering. Specifically he
couldn't stop thinking about her. She was a pregnant
woman, courtesy of his brother. Yet he couldn't wait
to go home and watch her move. Contemplate the
miracle of life growing inside her. Bask in the feminine mysteries of her presence and get to know the shy
but unconventional spirit he'd glimpsed in her amazing green eyes.

Don't be a fool, he thought, doing his best to focus
on the final plans for a free-form swimming pool that
would be poured the following afternoon. The bargain you struck with her constitutes the ideal marriage for someone with your history and disinclination
to trust. You don't want to ruin things.

Yet he'd been starved for company. Worked too
many hours and come home too many evenings to an
empty house. He couldn't push down his excitement

when he pulled into his parking space shortly after 6:00 p.m. to find her waiting for him on the porch.

Feigning nonchalance, he fixed them drinks—a rum concoction for him and ice-cold fruit juice for her. Too late he realized it had been a mistake to sit beside her on the swing. She kept stirring it with her foot and, as she exclaimed over the harbor view and demanded he name its various landmarks, the slight motion combined with her perfume to create an erotic effect.

Hold it right there, jocko, he ordered himself. Given her condition and your agreement, she's strictly off limits. To his chagrin, he found himself warming to her as a person as well.

Their conversation turned to the house and Ned explained that, during the early part of their marriage, his parents had lived on St. Lucia.

"At the time, Grandfather was running Balfour Shipping and he sent Oliver down here to acquire as many banana plantations as he could," he related. "Imported tropical fruit was becoming big business. I was about two then. We lived in a rented villa over in Vigie for a few months until my mother, Emily Balfour, got pregnant with Milo. That's when Oliver bought this house."

"You mean . . . Milo was born here?" Jenny asked.

Ned nodded, wishing he hadn't brought up the subject. "We didn't go back to England for several years," he added. "Since then, the place has served as a holiday rendezvous for us."

Jenny's eyes were bright with curiosity. "Then there must be some old pictures around," she speculated.

He shrugged, not guessing where she was headed. "I suppose there might be a few."

"I mean of Milo, when he was a baby."

Appalled, Ned didn't stop to think it might be love for the child she carried and eagerness for some clue to its appearance that had motivated her, not any lingering feelings for his brother. For him, it was as if an icy wind had withered the lush tropical evening, destroying its volatile unspoken promise.

Ronnie couldn't get Milo out of her system, either, he thought in disgust. She kept phoning him for months, long after he'd ceased wanting anything to do with her.

"Do me a favor," he said, abruptly getting to his feet. "Ask Arabella to bring my dinner into the study. Because of the time I spent picking you up at the airport this morning, I'm behind on my paperwork."

Chapter Five

That night, Jenny sat in solitary splendor at the Balfours' lovely old dining-room table, facing a filet of beef with vegetables she didn't want. Belatedly she was aware of what she'd done to shatter the delicate rapport she and Ned had begun to cultivate. As she stared into the flames that flickered inside a pair of crystal hurricane lamps, she wished to God she'd never opened her mouth.

She couldn't think of a way to put things right. When she'd mentioned Milo's baby pictures, it was as if Ned had slammed a door in her face.

I can hardly go to him and say, "Look, I don't give a damn about your brother," she acknowledged miserably. Though it's true, he wouldn't believe me. He'd just say it doesn't matter, provided I don't do anything to embarrass him.

Maybe in time he'd abandon the distrust that sprang from her connection with Milo and she'd be able to talk freely with him—explain herself if she was misunderstood. But Jenny wasn't willing to bet on it. She guessed her advancing pregnancy would be a constant reminder of what he probably considered her moral laxity and bad judgment. Despite his avowed eagerness to be a father, she couldn't bring herself to think about how he'd view the baby when it arrived.

I should have stayed in London, she thought, pushing her plate away and returning to the porch to watch an ethereal lavender sunset. Coming here and invading his privacy this way was a big mistake.

She barely saw Ned for the next several days. Each morning, he was dressed and gone before she made it to the breakfast table. Apparently he didn't bother with lunch. And, though they spoke briefly when he returned from work, there were no shared evening meals, no relaxed conversations on the porch.

Lonely and at loose ends, Jenny didn't want to become a prisoner in the house with a fascinating place such as St. Lucia at her doorstep. Lacking transportation of her own, she decided to begin exploring with the resort itself.

At first Ned objected to her daily jaunts on foot, expressing concern for the baby. Though it was obvious he continued to have misgivings, he fell silent on the subject when she brought him a note from her new obstetrician approving them.

Now and then their paths crossed. One afternoon, he waved to her from the restaurant roof, where he was checking the rustic wooden shingles workmen were nailing in place, and she returned the greeting. The next day they chatted a few minutes as he supervised the installation of several tennis courts.

Given his passion for exercise, it was inevitable they'd meet on the beach. One evening she'd walked a fair distance from the house and started back when he appeared, jogging toward her in running shoes and a pair of swimming trunks. As he paused to say hello, she tried not to notice the glistening muscles of his chest and shoulders.

To her surprise, instead of continuing his run, he decided to walk back with her. Little prickles of awareness feathered over her skin as he used a terry-cloth towel he'd tucked into his waistband to mop the sweat from his body.

The following evening, Ned decided to join her at the dinner table. Though he felt somewhat self-conscious at first, partaking of one of the rituals of married life with her, he had to admit she seemed pleased at his presence. We're company for each other, he rationalized, attempting to categorize his mixed emotions under a safe heading. Though we have nothing in common and we hail from opposite sides of the Atlantic, here on St. Lucia we're more alike than different.

Grateful the tension between them had eased, Jenny didn't push for anything more complicated. Her pregnancy and the far-reaching changes it had wrought in her life had left her feeling vulnerable, and there were times when she yearned with an almost physical ache for a shoulder to lean on. Yet she was convinced that, the minute she tried to appropriate his, he'd retreat. The bemused, questioning mood she'd sensed in him the day of her arrival seemed to have vanished like a puff of smoke.

Before leaving London, she'd availed herself of the charging privileges Ned had bestowed on her to purchase a few items of resort wear, including a maternity swimming suit. However, during her first two weeks on St. Lucia, she avoided the water, surmising from Ned's overprotective manner that he'd disapprove of her taking a dip.

The turquoise-and-sapphire bay that lapped at the resort's tan crescent of beach continued to beckon, however. One especially fine morning, she couldn't resist it any longer. Tossing a paperback novel, a tube of sunscreen and a beach towel into a straw tote and covering her suit with a colorful cotton shift in case she ran into her husband, she informed Arabella she wouldn't be back for lunch.

A steep flight of concrete steps across the road from the house was the most direct route to the beach, and Jenny decided to go that way. When she reached the sand, she tossed her espadrilles into the tote with her other things. The tide was up and, rolling hypnotically to shore, the breakers invited her. Sand crumbled pleasantly between her toes.

This is what I came to St. Lucia for, she tried to convince herself.

The spot she'd chosen for her swim was beyond the hotel and the new restaurant Ned was building by several hundred yards, and she started walking in that direction. Still in the process of renovation, the hotel hadn't been in operation for some time. There were no lifeguards or printed signs to warn her of a periodic undertow.

As she passed the shuttered charcoal shack Ned said had once dispensed island barbecue and light lunches to beach goers, she saw nothing but the flagpole she'd noticed the day of her arrival. Beneath the St. Lucian flag, a plain white banner was frequently displayed.

That morning, someone had changed it to red. She wondered at the significance.

A short time later she arrived at a stretch of beach along which—a dozen steps or so up the hillside—several clusters of luxury villas had been built. The sand was partially screened from the villas by sea grape, pandanus and a stand of geranium trees. Despite the nearby presence of workmen, who were putting the finishing touches to some of the villas' interiors, she felt it would be secluded enough.

Taking off her shift and placing it with her tote at the foot of a low, sandy embankment, she got her feet wet. The water felt wonderful—pleasantly cool and invigorating. Damp and charged with ionization from the spray, the air caressing her skin. The breakers appeared mild, frothy, nonthreatening.

Emboldened, Jenny ventured deeper. I'll only go out a little way, she promised herself. She was playing like a child in surf that broke just below her breasts when, with a sudden *whoosh,* a particularly powerful wave knocked her off her feet.

On her knees as another wave crashed over her, she found to her horror that she couldn't get up. One after another, the waves kept pounding her as she struggled to right herself. The undertow was fearsome in its strength.

Even the *sand* was tugging at her, dragging her seaward as it undermined her efforts. In a moment or two, she'd be out of her depth. *My baby!* she thought, hollow-throated with panic. What if I drown? Or injure him? Rolling in the surf like a stricken porpoise, she began to scream.

By chance, Ned had just arrived at one of the nearby villas where a prototype decorating treatment awaited his approval when her cries clutched at the air. Several of his workmen heard them, too, and started running to her assistance. In superb condition from years of regular exercise, Ned was faster. Hurtling down the steps to the beach, he dashed into the water. In just seconds, he was lifting Jenny in his arms.

Sobbing, she clung to him.

"Are you hurt?" he asked roughly, his dark eyes overflowing with concern and something akin to anger as he carried her to safety.

Her knees and elbows stung from the scouring they'd received as she'd tried to escape the breakers' pounding and her mouth and nose burned with salt water. But she was alive. In one piece. She hadn't consigned her baby to a watery death.

"N-no, I don't think so." She choked.

One of the workmen spread out a towel. Ned shook his head. "I'll take her up there," he said, nodding at the villa he'd been about to inspect.

Forcefully mounting the wooden steps that connected the new accommodations he'd built with the beach, Ned carried Jenny into the two-story villa's lower-floor bedroom. Heedless of its expensive new decorator covering, he deposited her on the king-size bed.

By now, the reality of what could have happened had sunk in, with chilling effect. Jenny shuddered. In response, Ned wrapped the bedspread around her. There was scant grace or tenderness in the gesture.

"You little fool," he said after a moment, glaring down at her. "Why did you go in with the red flag flying? You could have drowned in that undertow. Or at the very least had a miscarriage!"

Horrified comprehension dawned on Jenny's face. The red flag had signified danger. She'd behaved like an idiot, sneaking off without consulting him. As for the effects of her foolishness, they might not be counted yet.

"I had no idea what it meant," she whispered in a guilt-stricken voice.

His expression didn't change. "Well, now you do," he advised curtly, turning away and instructing one of his workmen to phone a doctor.

An expatriate Englishman, Jenny's obstetrician maintained an office near the Roman Catholic convent, on the far side of Castries. It was at least a fifteen-minute drive from the resort. However, an elderly general practitioner who'd been born on the island lived just up the road from them, where he operated a dispensary from his residence. The workman called him and he was on the scene in just a few minutes.

After examining Jenny in private, he called Ned back into the room. "As far as I can tell, your wife is none the worse for her mishap," he announced in his lilting eastern Caribbean cadence. "We'll know for certain in a few days. Meanwhile, if I were you, Mr. Balfour, I'd take her home, see to it she has a nice warm bath to relax her and put her to bed. For her baby's sake, she'd do well to rest for the next twenty-four hours."

Bundling Jenny up in the spread, which by now was wrapped around her inside out, Ned drove her back to the house in his Jeep and carried her up the front steps. To his chagrin, Arabella hadn't returned from marketing yet. There was no one but him to help his wife undress.

Irritated afresh at the prospect of enforced intimacy, he started to carry Jenny to her room.

"I can walk," she protested, thoroughly humiliated by all the trouble she'd caused and painfully aware his displeasure was justified.

A muscle tightened in his jaw. "If you insist."

At Ned's insistence, they took the stairs slowly, with his strong right arm supporting her. What's he planning to do... bathe me and tuck me into bed? she wondered with a little shiver when he entered her room instead of stopping at the door. She didn't need or want further assistance.

"If you could just turn on the shower and adjust the temperature, I'd appreciate it," she said, hoping that, by giving him something to do, she could avoid further embarrassment at his hands.

To her dismay, he insisted on peeling her suit down to her ankles as if she were a child. She burned with shame and an emotion she didn't care to name as his strong, impersonal fingers brushed her distended belly and engorging breasts.

How dreadful I must look to him, she thought, all swollen and shapeless with my hair clinging to my head like seaweed! Modesty was a corpse that would never recover. Like the swimsuit she'd put on with such pleasure that morning, her pride and integrity lay in an ignominious heap.

"Step free, damn it!" Ned prompted, losing patience with her as a direct result of his own formidable discomfort. "You needn't worry about shocking me," he added sarcastically. "I've seen naked women before."

Jenny complied, her cheeks burning. To her, his implication was crystal-clear. She had nothing to offer that he'd find the least bit tempting.

Already regretting his outburst, Ned wrapped an oversize towel around her shoulders. "Sit here on the bed until the shower's ready," he said more gently, disappearing into her private bath.

I'll never be able to stay here after this, she moaned silently, a tear running down her cheek as she did his bidding. Any possibility of a comfortable relationship between us has been irretrievably shattered. I might as well return to London and hope his involvement will keep him here until I'm old and gray.

The rushing sound of the shower carried to her and, a moment later, Ned returned to help her into the tub. Heartsick and a little unsteady on her feet now that her sense of crisis had abated, Jenny didn't drop her towel until she was safely behind the curtain.

"Thanks, I'm all right now. You can go back to work," she assured him, letting the warm spray surround her like a protective envelope.

His reply was as terse and stubborn as the man. "I'll be right here in case you need me."

She could see his blurred outline through the translucent curtain as, keeping his back to her, he took off his shirt and sodden loafers. I'm such a fool, she thought, crying a little more as she turned so that the spray was directed at her back. He has every right to be furious with me. I *could* have lost the baby....

With privacy and a chance to reflect, the doctor's casual words echoed in her ears. *We'll know for certain in a few days,* he'd said. She might not be out of danger yet.

Abruptly little lozenges of light swam before her eyes. "Ned," she called in a frightened voice, catching hold of the towel bar. "I'm feeling lightheaded...."

A split second later, he was in the tub with her, water soaking his already drenched khaki shorts and plastering his hair to his forehead as he pulled her into his arms. A pang of helplessness seized her as she realized their bodies were touching. Her breasts were crushed against his flat male nipples and dark tangle of chest hair.

Ned was every bit as aware of that extraordinary phenomenon as she was. "C'mon," he said, his voice going gruff as he stepped back slightly and reached for the shower controls. "Let's get back out of here before you pass out and really hurt yourself."

By now, Jenny's episode of vertigo had passed. She and the baby were probably going to be all right. She'd just have to take it easy for a few days.

Whatever else she felt for Ned, she knew he'd earned her trust. He was a tough, pragmatic but decent and caring man who'd built a wall around his heart—one who'd been hurt and didn't plan to trust again. At the thought that he'd known rejection, too, a surge of fatalism more powerful than any she'd ever experienced urged her not to let the moment end just yet.

"Please...don't," she said softly, staying his hand. "I'm okay now. I'm sure my dizziness was psychological, not physical. I realized that, if I'd gone into labor..." Her green eyes lost themselves in his brown ones as she contemplated the tragedy they'd escaped. "I'd never want to do anything to hurt our baby," she whispered.

Her choice of words slipped like a lance of sweetness into his thoughts. He knew without being told that it had been unpremeditated.

For a moment, his gaze intensified. Then, "Turn around," he directed. "I'll steady you."

Not answering, Jenny obeyed. As she gave herself up to the warm spray and incredible guarantee of his touch, she was transported to a sensual, almost dreamlike state. I must be crazy, she thought. I'm a mother-to-be, yet I'd give anything to have him touch me all over. How can I possibly feel this way?

His cheek inches from her hair, his lower body grazing the curve of her buttocks, Ned found their juxtaposition as mind-boggling as she did. He'd never seen a naked pregnant woman before, much less touched one, and now he was holding one in his arms.

Though he hadn't contributed the sperm that had set off the miracle of life in her, the child she'd bear would belong to him. He'd nurture and care for it, love it as she did. For one blazing moment unprecedented in his experience, he felt as if they were the only two people in the world. He didn't want the sensation to end, despite a jumble of darker, more primitive feelings he considered highly inappropriate.

Jenny didn't, either. For the first time since she could remember, she didn't feel as if she was alone in the world. Whatever Ned thought of her, she still had him. It was all she could do not to relax against him, let his warmth and solid strength flow into her pores.

At last she couldn't justify drawing out their intimacy any further. "You can turn off the water now, if you'd like, and hand me a towel," she suggested reluctantly, wishing she'd met him and not his brother first.

* * *

Following the incident at the beach and their impromptu tête-à-tête in the shower, Ned seemed especially distant. Jenny thought she understood. For the span of several minutes, their wordless communication had been so powerful they'd almost been able to think each other's thoughts. He'd made it clear he didn't want that kind of relationship with her.

She took comfort in the fact that there were no physical repercussions from her misadventure and the genuine concern Ned seemed to feel for her despite his unwillingness to let her get too close.

Late August rolled around and several airline executives and their spouses were scheduled to arrive for a visit. Ned had been negotiating with them to promote package tours once the resort was operational, and he'd invited them down to St. Lucia to check it out. Though he didn't plan to open for business until December, he'd arranged to put them up in several of the completed villas and provided limited food service. To that end, he'd hired a skeleton staff.

"I know you're almost seven months along and it might seem a bit onerous, but I wonder if I could enlist your aid," he said one evening at dusk as they shared an unaccustomed light supper on the porch. "It goes without saying that I'll entertain my VIP's royally while they're on St. Lucia...both here in our home and in several of the island's finer restaurants. I wonder if..."

Jenny hid her little rush of enthusiasm. "You'd like me to help."

He nodded. "If you wouldn't mind. You're my wife, after all. They'll expect it."

Up late, a sugar bird hopped on the rim of a fruit bowl Arabella had set out and pecked in desultory fashion at one of the miniature red bananas it contained as a small silence lengthened between them. Ned wants the world to think we're a normal married couple, Jenny concluded—even though that's not the case.

His back to the lights of Castries as they winked on in the deepening twilight, his face partially in shadow, he was waiting for her answer.

"All right...I'll help," she said, thinking what a strong sensual pull he exerted.

Despite getting herself into trouble with Milo, she'd had very little experience with the opposite sex. Yet she knew one thing with certainty. Ned was a man just made for loving. She wondered if there was a woman in the picture she didn't know about.

Chapter Six

Planned by Jenny and carried out with Arabella's help, the dinner party she and Ned hosted for his executives and their mates was an unqualified success. The table was dressed in heirloom china, tropical flowers and old silver. Candlelight puddled on hand-rubbed mahogany and flickered in the soft Caribbean breeze admitted by half-open floor-to-ceiling windows.

Everyone agreed the leg of lamb was superb, the wine that accompanied it perfection. Beginning with the hors d'oeuvres and continuing on through the dessert, talk flowed easily, bubbling into little swirls of laughter that eddied around the room.

Seated at the opposite end of the table, Jenny discreetly observed her husband. He looked pleased, even expansive as he chatted with their dinner guests. How nice it is to be able to do something for him, she thought. If it weren't for Ned, I'd be in Seattle tonight, scraping by on Aunt Etta's handouts or living alone in a run-down apartment, my food, rent and medical care paid for by the people who planned to adopt my baby.

In essence, he'd saved her from heartbreak. Yet for all his generosity and concern, at times she still felt herself to be something of a charity case. She was the necessary baggage that would allow him to have the child he wanted without investing anything of himself in another man-woman relationship.

Though they could have no earthly idea of the deal that had been struck, Jenny was convinced their female guests, at least, could sense their marriage wasn't typical. For all his courteous attention, even warmth toward her, there was nothing loving or intimate in Ned's manner. A kind of odd formality separated them.

The following evening, Ned treated the group to chicken curry, *pappadams* and patna rice with mango chutney at the Green Parrot Restaurant atop the Morne. It was still daylight out when they assembled on its red-tiled terrace, which overlooked the melting, almost Mediterranean beauty of Castries as seen from the heights, and went into the mural-decked bar for drinks.

They'd begun their revels early for a reason. Though Ned had tried to dissuade them, warning that it wouldn't be anything like what they expected, several of the executives' wives had insisted on sampling the famous "jump-up" or street fair held every Friday night in the tiny fishing village of Gros Islet. They'd read somewhere that it represented unspoiled, indigenous Caribbean culture at its best.

By the time they'd claimed their table by the restaurant's open-air windows and begun their meal, everyone except Jenny and perhaps Ned, who'd downed a single whiskey neat, was a little high on alcohol. Jenny, who'd abstained from anything stronger than Perrier with a twist for her baby's sake, didn't feel deprived. More relaxed with their guests now that she knew them better and delighted to be out for the evening with her husband, she was thoroughly enjoying herself.

Part of the reason was Ned's behavior. Instead of facing her from the opposite end of a formally set dining table, he was seated cozily next to her. As he conversed with the executive on her left, he rested one arm casually on the back of her chair. They were almost like a couple. I could get addicted to evenings like this, Jenny thought.

Over the crème caramel and bananas flambé, he leaned over to whisper something in her ear. "Sure you want to come with us to the street carnival, Jen?" he asked, drawing his dark brows together. "You've been a real trooper the past few days and I don't want to wear you out. If you like, I'll phone for a cab to take you back to the house."

Don't you want me along? she asked him silently, her effervescent mood stumbling. Or are you just expressing concern for me and the baby?

She decided to accept the latter explanation until it was proven inaccurate. "If you don't mind, I'd really like to go," she answered. "Your reluctance to take everyone has made me a little curious."

From the Green Parrot, they piled into a chauffeur-driven van owned by the resort for the short drive to Gros Islet. Seating was crowded but no one seemed to mind. There was a lot of joking and laughter. Pressed against one of the door handles, Ned put his arm around Jenny to conserve space.

Her eyes widened as she got her first look at their destination. Instead of getting out of the van to immerse themselves in a colorful, brightly lit festival featuring live reggae or calypso music and native crafts, they'd descend amid a jumble of dark, incredibly poor hovels. The sagging, unpainted scrap-lumber dwellings looked like subdivided boxcars, or packing crates.

"Derek Walcott calls them 'kneeling shacks,'" Ned observed, gauging her reaction with interest.

Courtesy of a book she'd found in the Balfour family's vacation library, Jenny had a nodding acquaintance with the writer he'd mentioned. A native St. Lucian, Walcott was known as the poet laureate of the Caribbean. "I can't think of a more apt description," she replied, overcome by the unbelievable poverty of it all.

Though their British visitors appeared shocked, too, they gamely insisted on being good sports. They'd try the local beer, maybe even dance a few numbers. Lacing his fingers firmly through Jenny's, Ned led the way. The shadowy, unpaved streets were crammed with parked cars, a crush of locals and tourists on foot. Village residents, including children, aggressively hawked beer and cheap T-shirts.

A pall of smoke from homemade charcoal grills laden with chicken joints and slabs of ribs, also for sale, hung over everything. To Jenny's disappointment, the only music was recorded. A deejay at one end of the street was blasting soul tunes from gargantuan speakers for a tightly knit, swaying group of

dancers. His selections were forced to compete with
the outpouring of noise from a host of boom boxes.

There was a separate dance to hard rock with sug-
gestive lyrics taking place in a weed-choked vacant lot.
A mixed group of dedicated boozers, ladies-of-the-
evening and Rastafarians in dreadlocks had congre-
gated outside a two-story building displaying a neon
advertisement for Cockspur Ale. Without question, it
was the village's most prosperous establishment.

A number of dubious-looking tourists had joined
them. The tourists clung to their crudely hammered-
together stools and rough tables outside the bar as if
they were life rafts and the mass of humanity roam-
ing Gros Islet's packed streets a highly dangerous
flood.

Jenny couldn't blame them. To her, the festival
looked like the perfect setup for drug dealers and
pickpockets, despite Ned's whispered comment that
there were probably quite a few plainclothes police-
men around. Attuned to protecting her unborn child,
she was reluctant to be jostled by the milling throng or
get separated from her husband. For once his overprotective ways meshed perfectly with her sentiments.

They entered the bar briefly so he could treat their
guests to a beer. Its decor was an eclectic mix of ad-
vertisements, calendar photos, the kind of mirrored
globe that usually graces a dance hall and various
items of sentimentalized religious art. Jenny noted a
representation on velvet of the Last Supper, a
wounded but magnanimous-looking Sacred Heart. In
a back room painted electric robin's-egg-blue, a group
of men were drinking and swearing as they played
cards.

"The folks back home in London are never going to believe this," one of their women companions predicted with a laugh as they went back outside and pushed their way along the crowded street toward the deejay's sphere of influence.

Beer bottles in hand, the airline executives and their mates quickly joined in the dancing. Jenny wasn't surprised when Ned made no move to follow their example. However, after a few dances and another beer or two, purchased from a slim young man in a ragged shirt who dispensed them from a portable picnic cooler, their guests had mellowed considerably. They demanded full participation.

"What do you say, Jen," Ned asked with obvious reluctance, glancing at her. "If you'd rather not..."

She had the perfect excuse if she wanted to let him off the hook. In her seventh month, she'd begun to feel full-blown, ungainly, as if she were carrying around a beach ball under her dress. Yet for once the deejay had selected a slow number. And she'd never danced with Ned. It might be quite a while before she had another chance.

"I guess one dance wouldn't hurt," she answered, not quite meeting his eyes.

Bowing to pressure from all sides, he took her in his arms and placed his right hand tentatively at the base of her spine. She rested her left hand on his shoulder. Considerably more prominent than it had been beneath her white linen shift the day of her arrival, her stomach pressed against him.

The shock of recognition was instantaneous for them both. Suddenly it was as if they were alone amid the crush of bodies. Their gazes had no option but to mesh, their senses none but to admit the truth. There, within the circle of touch, was the soul-absorbing *other* they'd each discovered in the mirrors aboard his London yacht and found again in a shower on St. Lucia.

I'm in love with him, Jenny realized in a flash of intuition that rocked her to the soles of her feet. He's everything his brother isn't and the answer to my girlhood dreams.

For his part, Ned was drowning in conflicting emotions. Every latent vulnerability he possessed had come rushing to the surface. I don't want this, he thought, on the verge of pushing her away even as the sensual man in him drew her closer and rested his cheek against her hair.

Though their guests laughed and talked in the van on their way back to the resort, Jenny and Ned said very little. Not a word passed between them after they left their passengers off and rode the short distance up the bluff to their house.

It was only after Ned had helped her out of the van and given her a hand up the front steps that he paused and asked if she'd like to have a drink with him.

"I suppose so," she agreed in a small voice. "I could stand a glass of milk."

Arabella had gone home for the night and Ned fetched Jenny's milk along with a whiskey for himself. Seated at opposite ends of the porch swing, they sipped and rocked quietly for several minutes as she waited for him to speak.

"I just wanted to thank you for acting as hostess tonight," he told her at last. "And for making our dinner party last night such a resounding success. I know that sort of thing wasn't part of our original agreement."

Stung, Jenny realized his words had a none-too-subtle message. As far as he was concerned, they'd made a deal. He expected them both to stick to it.

"You're more than welcome," she managed to say, heartsore and determined not to show it. "It wasn't any trouble. Since I'm pretty tired, I guess I'll say good-night."

The following morning, in the small work space he'd established at the hotel, Ned took his twice-weakly call from his father. Oliver reported he was suffering few angina symptoms despite putting in half days three times a week at the main office at Balfour Shipping in Ned's stead.

They discussed business at some length, with Nigel Carstairs adding a few comments from an extension phone. Finally, about to sign off, Oliver mentioned that Milo had accompanied him into the city and would like a word with Ned.

The latter was stunned when his brother inquired about Jenny's welfare. He couldn't keep a note of sarcasm out of his voice. "She's fine," he said shortly. "I didn't know you cared."

There was a brief silence. "And the baby?" Milo asked.

Ned could feel a strong sense of outrage building in his gut. Milo hadn't wanted the child he'd given Jenny and now that child was his. He'd be damned if he'd cede his brother a part-time interest.

"According to Jennifer's obstetrician, her infant is developing normally," he snapped. "Does that about do it? I'm not inclined to discuss this subject any further with you."

Again the satellite connection hummed empty for a moment.

"I, uh, just wondered, you know," Milo said somewhat sheepishly at last. "If you happen to think of it, tell her I wish them well."

His suspicions aroused that Milo might have undergone a change of heart because Pam had jilted him or he saw some benefit in being acknowledged as the parent of Oliver's first grandchild, Ned didn't pass on the message. A few days later, he and Jenny were at breakfast on the porch when an unexpected visitor arrived. It was Viv Balfour's thirty-year-old son from a former marriage, Howie Chappell, a St. Lucia land agent.

Introducing himself to Jenny before Ned had an opportunity to do the honors, the sandy-haired, freckle-faced Howie helped himself to generous portions of Arabella's scrambled eggs with sausage, fresh papaya and powdered-sugar-dusted "bakes" or flat St. Lucian fried doughnuts, without waiting for an invitation and joined them at the table.

"Howie grew up here," Ned said, quirking one brow as their impromptu guest dug in. "In fact, Oliver and Viv met on St. Lucia during a vacation he took after my mother died. Viv's the one who got him interested in redoing this place."

Throughout Ned's remarks, the ginger-haired Howie continued to shovel in the food. Finally, his initial appetite appeased, he paused to question Ned about several banana plantations he'd heard might be on the market.

From what Jenny could tell, though there wasn't any animosity between the two men such as that which separated Ned and his brother, her husband wasn't overly fond of Viv's son. He seemed to regard Howie as a mild form of nuisance. She got the distinct impression he was being less than candid where the banana plantations were concerned.

After Ned left, ostensibly to supervise some improvements he'd ordered for the golf course, Howie availed himself of seconds and remained behind to chat with her. Before long, he'd extracted her place of birth, educational background and reason for traveling to London. Eager to cut off the flow of questions before he asked how she and Ned had happened to meet, Jenny maneuvered him back to his original topic.

"It must be fun to travel around the island in your work, visiting banana plantations and the like," she remarked ingenuously. "I've been on St. Lucia since early July, and I've never laid eyes on one, let alone caught a glimpse of those fabulous mountains you call The Pitons."

His blue eyes registering surprise, Howie took the bait. "Old Ned's been remiss, I see," he answered, wiping his mouth. "Well, you know what they say about 'all work.' It makes one a dull boy. Tell you what...I'm off to La Resource and Mabouya, a banana-growing area, this morning. I might get as far as Dennery. If you'd like to ride along..."

Jenny knew Ned would disapprove of such a jaunt. The roads were rough—as Nigel Carstairs had said—and she and Howie had barely met.

Yet he *was* a kind of relative. Agonizing over her discovery that she loved Ned and his subsequent rejection of her, though conversely he'd seemed a bit more approachable since their talk on the porch swing, she decided she'd like nothing better than a tour of the island. It would free her temporarily from her thoughts.

She'd come to the breakfast table that morning in a modest nightgown and pink-striped cotton robe. "Give me a moment to change and I'll be right with you," she told her husband's stepbrother, jumping up from the table and going upstairs to put on a flowered shift.

The highway from Castries to Dennery, a medium-size town on St. Lucia's windswept Atlantic coast, snaked around mountains, skirted a rain forest and dipped into numerous valleys lush with banana plantings. Each fold between steep slopes contained a veritable sea of banana stalks, tender, oversize leaves and unripe fruit swathed in blue plastic.

The road's surface was pocked with craters, and Howie and Jenny were held up periodically by resurfacing projects. Travel was slow. Yet the scenery was worth it. To Jenny, the tiny banana-growers' huts, ebony-skinned children waiting for the bus in their colorful school uniforms and deep, junglelike valleys were fascinating. The rural landscape made her think of the way she'd always pictured Tahiti. If only Ned had offered to show it to her.

Unfortunately the road was even rougher than she'd anticipated and she was beginning to feel uncomfortable from all the jostling. She'd also realized that, though as the crow flew the distance wasn't very great, their round-trip would take much longer than she'd expected.

For some reason, since the night of the street fair, Ned had made a habit of coming home for lunch. At the rate they were going, she'd never make it back in time. And she hadn't left him a note. She wondered if she'd be able to locate a telephone.

As they drove, Howie switched on the radio. Treated to a Bob Marley tune and something with unintelligible lyrics by a local band, they suddenly found themselves listening to a spate of funeral announcements. The list of family members, friends and affiliations that accompanied each deceased person's name seemed endless.

"Does everyone on St. Lucia have that many relatives?" Jenny asked in amazement.

Howie grinned. "Actually a lot of people do if you count a man's *dou-dou's* and all the children he's had with them."

"What's a *dou-dou?*" she said, fairly certain she'd already guessed.

"Girlfriend, mistress, wife without benefit of matrimony," her husband's stepbrother instructed. "In the Caribbean, that kind of thing is commonplace."

At last they turned down the rutted dirt road that led to an overseer's shack at one of the plantations Howie planned to visit. Jenny's heart sank when she spotted Ned's Jeep parked beside a cherry-red Wagoneer. Tanned and muscular in his khaki shorts and a white polo shirt, her husband was conferring with an elderly gentleman whose features were shaded by a broad-brimmed straw hat.

"Damn," Howie muttered. "I should have known better than to mention this place to him."

It was suddenly clear to Jenny that he and her husband were interested in buying the same properties. After learning of Howie's intentions at the breakfast table, Ned hadn't let any grass grow under his feet.

Catching sight of her in Howie's company, he looked anything but agreeably surprised. With apologies to his companion, he broke off their conversation and came striding over to them.

"What are you doing here?" he demanded under his breath, barely nodding in his stepbrother's direction as he helped Jenny to her feet. "I thought you told me you were going to be careful after your little misadventure at the beach."

With its reference to what she considered a serious lapse of judgment on her part, the comment hurt. Meanwhile, it was obvious she and Howie had interrupted something important. Once again I've made a fool of myself, she thought.

Taking hold of her arm, Ned walked her over to meet his elderly friend, leaving Howie to bring up the rear. "Max, this is my wife, Jennifer," he said with barely concealed annoyance. "Jen, Max Sonnenschein. He owns this place."

They remained just long enough for Max to tell Jenny that the growers who worked for him cultivated thirty of the island's one hundred and twenty-seven varieties of bananas and explain that the bright blue plastic bags she saw had been tied over the developing "hands" of fruit to keep the birds from eating them.

As soon as it was polite to do so, Ned announced their departure. Pointedly failing to include Howie in the invitation, he asked Max to join them for dinner at their home later that week, at which time he proposed they finalize their business transaction.

"No matter what anybody says, Max," he concluded, shaking hands with the aging plantation owner, "I'll see to it that you get the best price."

Minutes later, he and Jenny were in the Jeep, on their way back to the resort. Though he pointed out a few sights and named some of the more exotic vegetation, the trip was marked by extended silences. Jenny withdrew into herself.

Having shied away from personal involvement with her, neglected to show her around and left her to fend largely for herself, Ned was still jealous that she would go off with another man. Even the fact that it was Howie didn't make him feel any better.

Face facts, he told himself irritably. The agreement you made gives her carte blanche to consort with whomever she pleases, as long as it isn't your brother. It was just that he hadn't expected her to be so restless and independent while she was carrying the baby.

She's been much too cavalier about her welfare *and* our child's, he thought, justifying his mood. I've got to make sure it doesn't happen again. When they reached the house, he paused long enough to deliver a lecture.

To Jenny's surprise, it included a concession.

"As your husband, I'd prefer that you stay here in Castries, close to medical help, until the baby comes," he said, his brown eyes boring into hers from behind dark glasses. "However, if you must gallivant about the island, I'll take you myself."

Chapter Seven

September slipped into what passed for autumn south of the Tropic of Cancer, and St. Lucia's climate took a turn for the wet. In addition to the sun-laced showers that had blown up, seemingly from nowhere, and as quickly dissipated almost every afternoon since Jenny's arrival, a series of tropical waves spawned off Africa's west coast and brought with them spates of wind and rain.

Dry, sunny days became doubly precious to Ned, offering his best chance to complete the exterior work necessary to whipping the resort into shape. Yet he didn't let his urge to make the most of them interfere with keeping his promise to Jenny. As good as his word, he took her on a Wednesday picnic to historic Pigeon Point and, the following Saturday, an excursion to the Castries market.

Nibbling a sandwich as they gazed across the water to Cap Estate and strolling past stalls of fruit, spices and crafts in the cavernous covered market while Ned taught her the fine art of refusing local tradesmen without giving offense, Jenny felt protected if not cherished. He didn't love her and he probably never would. Yet it was comforting, now that her pregnancy had advanced to the point where people stared at her with interest, to have a visible and supportive husband.

One evening, he came home early and whisked her off for a tour of the college grounds atop the Morne. From a knoll where a British regiment had once defeated the French, Jenny was able to see Mount Gimie and catch her first longed-for glimpse of the distant Pitons to the south. Castries was a toy town spread out at their feet. A cruise ship looked as if it belonged in a bottle as it inched toward Pointe Seraphine.

"Ned, *thank you*," she said with feeling. "You can't imagine what a thrill it is to see the island from this perspective."

From the beginning, their marriage had been a business arrangement. Abandoned by Milo, she'd traded shared parenthood of her child for Ned's good name and the security he could provide. Apart from polite murmurs in response to routine courtesies on his part, she'd never thanked him for anything.

He lifted one brow in acknowledgment. How little it takes to make her happy, he thought, recalling his efforts to contain Ronnie's restlessness with diamonds and furs. A zealot when it came to her figure, which she'd claimed was part of her stock-in-trade as a television hostess, his ex-wife had refused even to consider letting a tiny new life take precedence over her waistline. By no stretch of the imagination could Ned picture her settling down to wait for an infant's birth, like a field of grain slowly ripening, the way Jenny had.

"If we're still here after the baby's born, I'll take you to see the Pitons by boat," he said impulsively.

Surprised and touched, Jenny got a distinct lump in her throat. "I'd love that," she whispered.

They regarded each other in silence for a moment.

"Do you think we will?" she asked. "Stay here that long, I mean."

A bit shaggier than he'd kept it in London, Ned's dark hair ruffled in the breeze as he considered her question. There was still a lot of work to do if the resort was to open as planned at the beginning of the winter season. Yet he'd recently hired a manager. Most of the supervision could be delegated. It was a matter of hours to fly between London and Castries.

Why had he stayed on, overseeing the job personally? Have I tired of the rat race that much? he asked himself. Desperately needed a change of pace?

Seldom heard or attended to, the voice of his inner man replied that Jenny's presence in his life was largely responsible for his waning sense of urgency. She'd slowed him down. Given him something to focus on besides progress and balance sheets. Dedicated achiever and wary husband-in-name-only that he was, he'd learned to trust to a mild form of contentment.

"We might," he answered, searching her face. "Would that bother you? If you'd feel more comfortable having the baby in London..."

The very last thing Jenny wanted was to return to England without Ned. If she never had to face Milo again or endure the tepid welcome given her by Viv and Oliver, it would be too soon for her. Meanwhile, in a way she couldn't quite put her finger on, she and

Ned had adjusted to each other. From their starting point as strangers who felt awkward as man and wife, they'd become companions of a sort—partners who would love and nurture the same precious baby.

"No," she said. "I wouldn't. I was just curious, that's all."

Later, as she rocked gently on the porch while Ned went over some cables from his father, Jenny ruminated about what it had been like to grow up in Seattle without loving parents. No memories like that lie in wait for you, my little one, she promised her unborn child. Both your mother and father love you. And want you very much.

By now it was almost unthinkable that a man other than Ned had planted the seed of a baby in her, though they'd never so much as kissed, let alone made love. The nightmarish scene in which she'd clumsily tried to fend off Milo's advances had become less a reality than a bad dream.

Soon, baby, soon... I'll be holding you in my arms and kissing your downy head, she thought. It's hard to believe that, if it weren't for your daddy, I might have been forced to give you up to strangers.

Sometimes she wondered if it was the way Ned had rescued her from such a bleak fate that made her love him so much. But she knew her feelings went much deeper than that. From the very first, something in her had reached out to the man himself in all his toughness and vulnerability.

Maybe when she was slim again and their baby was sleeping peacefully in the cradle one of Ned's workmen had made for him out of island mahogany, Ned would catch fire with wanting her. She'd take his need and gladly if it was the most he could give. As she rocked and gazed at the exotic view that had become so familiar to her, she dreamed of blurring and blending into the mystery of the man she loved.

Jenny was nearly eight months pregnant in mid-October when her St. Lucian idyll threatened to turn into a battle with the elements. One of the low-pressure systems that had continued to drift westward toward the Caribbean basin evolved into a tropical depression and then into a named storm. Christened Darryl, it continued to intensify and become better organized. It was about to reach hurricane strength.

According to TV weather reports relayed by satellite from the United States, Darryl's behavior was somewhat erratic. A meteorologist with the National Hurricane Center speculated that its eye would pass several hundred miles to the north of them. But it was really too early to tell. A weaker low off the coast of Venezuela bore watching. If it shifted, Darryl might change course, begin to move in a more westerly direction. The windward islands of St. Lucia, Barbados and St. Vincent could be a target.

Concerned, Ned halted his interior finishing projects and put his crews to work filling sandbags and constructing storm shutters. He also worried about Jenny.

"Maybe I should send you up to Miami before it's too late," he told her with a frown one evening after watching the latest update. "It would only be for a couple of weeks. I don't want you to have the baby here, at the height of a hurricane."

Rebellious at the prospect of being parted from him, Jenny dug in her heels. "I'm not due for six weeks," she argued. "Besides, you might be sending me directly into the storm's path. You know they're saying this one is unpredictable.''

Ned was silent a moment. "What about England, then?" he suggested. "Or Seattle? *It's* not likely to be in much danger. I'm sure you have a great many friends you'd like to visit there."

Jenny thought of Aunt Etta and her former colleagues who taught in the King County school system, most of whom were busy with their own lives. If she went into labor in the city where she'd been raised, in essence, she'd be alone.

"That *would* be packing me off to the ends of the earth," she said lightly, attempting to whitewash her stubbornness. "I don't want to leave...or switch doctors again at this late date."

Still skeptical, Ned didn't push. Moving closer, the storm intensified. Soon its top winds were gusting to more than ninety miles an hour. As they monitored its progress via the movement of a small, rotor-shaped symbol on TV weather charts and studied radar patterns that revealed an increasingly well-defined center, the low off South America shifted. A day later they learned Darryl had changed course, turning west-northwest.

The day after that it stalled. Big enough now to suck up all the disturbed weather from a wide radius, it left St. Lucia basking in the sun. Yet conditions weren't typical. The sky was streaked with unusual bands of cirrus clouds.

"La calme avant l'orage," a workman from Martinique commented, tipping his cap to Jenny as she took her morning walk.

With the aid of her college French, she translated. It was the calm before the storm.

Two days later, having strengthened again during its extended sojourn over open water, the hurricane resumed its westward course. Big and clumsy with her growing child, who'd begun to kick like a mule each night when she got into bed, Jenny was sleeping fitfully. She awoke from particularly restless dreams to find that the barometer had dropped. The sky was dull and overcast, the atmosphere tense.

Going down to breakfast, she learned from Arabella that Ned had already left the house. The pretty, young housekeeper was obviously on edge. "They say the hurricane is coming here," she announced worriedly in her musical West Indian accent. "That he gets stronger and stronger. You think, missus, it's all right if I go home to my family in Micoud for a few days?"

Jenny knew without being told that Ned wouldn't like it. He'd mentioned more than once that he found it reassuring, with her so close to term, to have another woman in the house. On the other hand, family was important to Arabella, especially her younger brothers and sisters, some of whom were still quite young. Her desire to watch over them was admirable.

I don't see what it could hurt to let her go, Jenny thought. I've got more than a month left. Insisting she stay here will only make her unhappy. It won't protect me from anything.

"I guess so," she said at last, earning a wide smile of gratitude. "Just make sure we have plenty of drinking water on hand before you go, okay? And put out the extra batteries and candles."

Helping herself to hot tea and some fresh papaya the housekeeper had prepared for her, she went out on the porch. Already the surf was up. On the pole by the charcoal shack, the St. Lucian flag and red warning banner snapped smartly in a stiffening breeze. The graceful fronds of the coconut palms that fringed the beach lashed at their trunks similar to those in a Winslow Homer watercolor.

Maybe the storm will bring us closer, Jenny mused, contemplating the bustle of activity her husband was directing. I've heard that can happen when people weather a crisis together. A moment later, she was thoroughly ashamed of herself. Hurricanes caused a great deal of damage. Lives and property were lost.

Chastened, she went back into the house and switched on the television. Though weathermen were predicting the storm's center would pass between Antigua and Guadeloupe, St. Lucia and the surrounding islands could expect to be buffeted by counterclockwise winds. They'd definitely feel its wrath.

By midafternoon, Arabella had gone, waving a guilt-ridden but relieved goodbye from a cousin's pickup truck. The island's schools and most of its government offices had closed. Uniformed civil defense volunteers swung into action, evacuating low-lying areas and urging residents by means of loudspeaker trucks to return to their homes and/or seek high ground. Most of the island's commercial shipping had left port several days earlier. Yachts and smaller seagoing craft had been secured or hauled into dry dock.

Jenny hadn't seen Ned since the night before. With the house so quiet, the lowering skies, increased velocity of the wind and dropping barometric pressure began to get on her nerves. She literally jumped when one of her husband's workmen knocked at the front door to say he'd been sent to nail their storm shutters into place. He'd just completed his task when the first raindrops started to fall.

With the shutters closed, the house was dark and airless. Fortunately those that covered the floor-to-ceiling windows leading from the living room to the porch bolted from the inside. Ned had instructed they be left open a crack, so she'd have some air. Yet she couldn't help feeling claustrophobic as the rain's tattoo quickened to a downpour.

She didn't bother to switch on a lamp, and Ned found her sitting in the gloom when he returned home shortly after 4:00 p.m. "Where's Arabella?" he asked.

Jenny hesitated. "I let her go home to Micoud."

He frowned, then shrugged off the irritation he felt. He was tired—literally exhausted from his labors of the past few days. But that wasn't any excuse to bark at his wife. His hard gaze softened. "We can get along without her, I suppose."

In response to Jenny's instructions, Arabella had filled several large cooking pots with water. Ned doubted it would be enough. In his experience, it sometimes took days to recertify a water supply after a hurricane had passed. Just in case, he filled the kitchen sink and the tub in Jenny's bathroom where he'd steadied her beneath the spray. He also got out a battery-operated radio and checked the hurricane lamps, so they'd be ready if—and probably when—the power failed.

At last there was nothing to do but wait. Returning to the living room, he bolted the remaining shutters and switched on a lamp. "Hungry?" he asked, glancing at Jenny over his shoulder as he fixed himself a rum and tonic at the liquor cart.

She shook her head.

He could almost sense her nervousness. "I should have sent you to Miami while there was still time," he said, opening a Perrier and pouring it over ice before handing it to her. "If anything happens to you or the baby, I'll never forgive myself."

Jenny's chin lifted, hinting at the resilience he'd come to expect. "This is where I want to be," she answered. "Nothing bad's going to happen to us."

She'd curled up in one corner of the couch and, to her surprise, he kicked off his loafers and joined her, propping his feet on the eighteenth-century reproduction coffee table. Bared by his khaki shorts, one of his tanned, muscular thighs was just inches from her toes.

A little tongue of warmth curled to life inside her. It wasn't overtly sexual. Yet she knew that, after the baby came, she'd yearn for him with all her strength. He was so contradictory, so special with his tough exterior and giving heart. For perhaps the millionth time since meeting him, she wondered what had caused him to build such a wall around his emotions.

"Have you ever been through a hurricane before?" she asked, taking refuge from her thoughts.

As the wind's howl increased and rain beat against the roof, Ned told her about a storm that had hit St. Lucia when he, Milo and Margaret were adolescents vacationing on the island with their family. Hoping to take the edge off her fears, he went on to speak of his college days. He even let her persuade him to offer a few insights into his failed first marriage.

Though he didn't divulge Ronnie's affair with Milo, Ned described his ex-wife's materialism and shared the disappointment he'd felt when she hadn't wanted children. "Now that I'm older and wiser," he said, "I realize things worked out for the best. Divorce would have been hard on them.''

Understanding a little better why Ned wanted to raise his brother's baby as his own, Jenny still couldn't fathom his reasons for avoiding emotional intimacy. Lots of people got divorced and went on to love again. There had to be more to the situation than he was willing to tell.

Rain hammered the shutters as the afternoon wore into evening. They heard the sound of a siren somewhere. The wind was like a big hand, pushing at the house. To distract Jenny, Ned brought up the idea of buying a town house when they returned to London.

''St. Katherine Dock is ideal for a bachelor, yachtsman or childless couple,'' he said. ''And I'll miss it, as it's been convenient to my work. However, with a little one to think about, I'd like to find something a bit roomier in the West End...near one of the great parks so his nanny can take him out for a breath of air. Would that suit you, Jen?''

Despite the sudden crash of a tree limb in the yard and the unnerving rattle of a loose shutter, Jenny smiled. ''Having a place near one of the parks would suit me to perfection,'' she answered. ''As for a nanny, let's wait and see. I plan to spend a lot of time with this baby myself.''

Again Ned noted how different she was from Ronnie, who'd have taken every available out if she'd been trapped into motherhood. Though he didn't say so, he resolved to delegate more responsibility so that he, too, could spend as much time as possible with their son or daughter. Nothing like flying in the face of Balfour tradition, he thought.

Stretching, he got up and turned on the television for a weather update. Seconds later, the screen went black. So did all the lights. The ceiling fan slowed and drifted to a standstill.

"Oh, no," Jenny exclaimed softly, surprised by the depth of panic she felt over a simple power failure. Maybe it was her condition, but the storm was beginning to get to her.

Ned got to his feet. "You know we've been expecting this," he said, switching on a pocket-size flashlight and using it to locate the matches. "What did you think the hurricane lamps and battery-powered radio were for?"

He could be direct, as she knew full well. Embarrassed, she didn't answer as he moved around the room, lighting the lanterns and switching on the radio. After her refusal to let him send her away to a place of safety, she must seem like an idiot. She was stunned a moment later when he returned to the couch and put one arm around her.

In the chiaroscuro of light and shadow, his expression was difficult to read at best. Yet one thing seemed certain. He wasn't as put out with her as she'd thought. If he *had* been, he wouldn't have offered himself as a refuge.

Tremulously she relaxed against him. Her senses reeled with his after-shave's crisp scent, the fresh, clean-laundered aroma of his casual garments. His body's muscular warmth drew her like a magnet.

What would he think if he knew how I felt about him? she asked herself, resting one hand lightly against his shirtfront. Has he guessed at some subliminal level that I want him to be my friend, my protector...in a sense, the father I never knew? That I ache to know him as a lover after the baby comes? In her heart, he already was those things... all the men she'd always missed.

Screaming like a troupe of banshees, Darryl's worst winds arrived around 8:00 p.m. The Balfours' home away from home, which had been built of tropical hardwoods in the early years of the nineteenth century, groaned and creaked beneath their onslaught. But it didn't succumb.

They were far enough above the waterline that they didn't have to worry about a storm surge engulfing them. Basking in Ned's nearness and lulled by his quiet strength, Jenny felt almost safe in the shuttered, high-ceilinged room where he'd once played as a boy. She was even a little sleepy, though she shuddered now and then at a thump or crashing sound as tree branches and debris blew against the house. As a result, she was doubly alarmed when Ned mentioned he ought to go outside and have a look around.

"You can't be serious," she said.

Gently he disengaged himself. "I'm afraid so. The resort's my responsibility."

Her brow puckered with worry, she followed him into the kitchen. Snatching up a slicker from a hook next to the pantry, he put it on, unbolted the back door and turned the handle. Nothing happened. Swearing, he pushed with all his strength.

Though the hurricane pushed back, he managed to get the door open. "Stand back, Jen!" he shouted, struggling out to the porch in a blast of rain, wind and debris.

Seconds later, the door had shut behind him. What if he doesn't come back? Jenny agonized, racing to one of the windows and trying without success to see what he was doing through the cracks between the shutters. What if he's injured and I can't help?

It seemed an eternity before he reappeared. Drenched to the skin, his dark hair plastered to his head as he stumbled back inside, he accepted the towel she handed him without comment. Though he'd sustained a cut above one brow as if he'd been nicked by flying glass, it didn't look to be that serious.

"What's it like out there?" she whispered as he dabbed at it and blotted up the wet.

He gave her a lopsided grin. "Not exactly what you'd call hospitable. From what I could tell, the hotel seems to be holding its own. Ditto the restaurant, though we'll probably have to replace the roof. There's a fishing boat docked in the middle of the charcoal shack. Do you suppose you could rustle up something to eat while I go upstairs and put on some dry clothes?"

When he came back down, he was barefoot. His hair had been slicked back with a comb and there was a flesh-colored bandage over his cut. He'd changed to tan trousers and a navy polo shirt. Jenny had spread their repast on the coffee table. They didn't talk much as they consumed cold curried chicken and fruit.

Afterward, Ned suggested she get some rest.

What Jenny wanted was his arm around her again, the unbelievably sweet sensation of nestling against him. "With all the wind and rain, I don't think I could sleep," she protested.

"You ought to try. I'll be right here. I won't go anywhere without telling you."

Flashlight in hand, she trudged upstairs against her will. Swept by its concentrated beam, her room was awash in shadows, a grotesque, alien place. Fierce guests of wind rattled the shutters. I don't want to be alone tonight, she thought as she undressed and put on a flower-sprigged nightgown. I want to be with him.

Ned was sprawled on the couch, wondering if he'd have to postpone their December opening. A lot would depend on how much damage the rest of the island had suffered. Tourists didn't want to spend their winter vacations in a tropical paradise that had been stripped of its exotic greenery, watching carpenters and other workmen make repairs.

He glanced up in surprise as Jenny padded into the room. She hadn't bothered to put on a robe. In the half-light, he could see the ripe outline of her stomach, the faint smudges of her nipples through her gown's thin fabric. Its hem stopped short of her knees, reminding him once again that she had slim, shapely legs.

"Something wrong?" he asked.

"I don't want to stay up there by myself."

An expression she couldn't fathom flickered in his eyes and was quickly hidden. "You have to rest, Jen," he insisted with a little shake of his head.

Though she didn't answer, she refused to budge.

Giving in to an urge he didn't care to examine too closely, Ned got to his feet. "C'mon," he growled, guiding her back to the stairs with a light touch between her shoulder blades. "If you think it'll help, I'll lie down with you."

Chapter Eight

Jenny's eyes sought Ned's as she turned back the lightweight coverlet and got into bed. She couldn't name the emotion that gazed back at her from their enigmatic depths and she wondered if he'd changed his mind. Apparently he hadn't. With a little shrug, as if freeing himself from scattered thoughts, he took off his navy polo shirt, unzipped his trousers and laid them over a chair. A moment later, he got in beside her wearing his boxer shorts.

During their visit to his family's estate immediately after their marriage, he'd slept on the couch. Now, after being husband and wife for five months, they were finally sharing a bed.

"Ned?" she whispered.

He drew her head against his shoulder. "Hush, Jen. Go to sleep. I'll watch over you."

Incredibly, as the storm raged, punishing St. Lucia with the back of its hand, Jenny felt herself courting stray wisps of dreams. She was big with his brother's child and he had no stake in her other than the baby. Yet she'd never felt so cared for, so safe. Not even a hurricane could harm her when she was in his keeping.

Ned's emotions were less tranquil, more difficult to define. It bothered him more than he could say to realize how utterly *right* it felt, to be lying in Jenny's bed with her soft, regular breathing grazing his chest. Even as big as a house, as she'd laughingly described herself several days earlier, she was fragile, sweet-smelling, quintessentially feminine. It had been a long time since he'd slept cozy between the sheets with a woman in his arms.

What you and she have is a business arrangement, he reminded himself. Not an open-ended friendship that might develop into something more sensual and profound. For you to be attracted to her isn't even seemly. She's carrying your brother's child, for God's sake.

What he needed was a good roll in the hay, with no strings attached. Yet he knew he wouldn't seek relief from the tension he felt—at least not yet. His understanding with Jenny that they'd each be free to pursue life's pleasures notwithstanding, taking another woman to bed while she was pregnant would feel like cheating on his marriage vows. As he rejected the idea, his feeling of closeness to her deepened. Despite her unfortunate connection to Milo, it began to heal a stubborn place in his heart.

By morning, the storm had passed. Rising at dawn and showering in his own bath so he wouldn't wake Jenny, Ned toured the damage with his new manager,

Brian Ladreau. The latter took copious notes as his boss ticked off the needed repairs.

Despite Darryl's fury, the devastation wasn't all that extensive. They'd lost some shingles, a number of plantings, the charcoal shack and several sailboats. The ground floor of the hotel, which was below the lobby level, had been flooded with seawater. Some of the storm shutters they'd built had come loose and there were a number of broken windows.

Most of their labor would involve cleanup. Like a juvenile delinquent, the hurricane had trashed and muddied what it couldn't destroy. Offering top dollar for additional help, Ned organized his crews and got them started right away. The fledgling Balfour Beach Hotel and Resort had received a healthy stack of reservations for its grand opening and he had no intention of canceling them.

With so much to do, he didn't make it back to the house until after 11:00 p.m. To his surprise, Jenny was waiting up for him. Arabella hadn't returned and, in the housekeeper's absence, she'd taken advantage of restored electrical power to prepare a shrimp creole with rice, which she was keeping warm on the back of the stove.

Exhausted though he was from his busy day, Ned was in an excellent mood. In his view, he had the repair-and-cleanup effort well in hand.

"The shrimp looks great," he said enthusiastically, lifting the lid on one of the cooking pots and peering inside. "But you needn't have gone to so much trouble."

Jenny's mouth curved. She hadn't often seen the boyish side of him. "I like to cook," she answered.

"And I didn't have anything else to do this afternoon."

As before, they ate in the living room. Ravenous, Ned polished off seconds yet managed to do most of the talking as he filled Jenny in on the damage the resort had sustained. By the time they'd finished, it was almost midnight—definitely time to call it a day. Yet neither of them suggested it. Jenny wondered if Ned was asking himself the same question she was: Would they continue to share a bed?

If so, she knew instinctively that he wouldn't mention it. If she wanted to hold on to the ground she'd gained with him, *she'd* have to bring up the subject.

At last they couldn't justify lingering over the decaffeinated coffee she'd brewed another second. Yawning, Ned proposed they carry their dirty dishes into the kitchen and stack them on the drain board. Hopefully Arabella would return in the morning to wash them. He didn't want Jenny spending too much time on her feet during the final month of her pregnancy.

It was now or never. Summoning her courage, she rested one hand on his arm. "Last night," she said softly. "I slept better than I have for a month despite the storm. I wonder if you'd consider..."

Ned's brown eyes were unreadable. "Spending another night in your bed?"

She nodded.

Something softened in his face. Despite her slender build, in the nightgown and robe she'd been wearing when he returned home, Jenny looked ready to deliver at any moment. He could only guess how uncomfortable she must be. Lately he'd had to stifle an urge to wait on her hand and foot. Under no such self-imposed compunction, apparently, she'd felt free to cook for him.

With uncharacteristic tenderness, he smoothed an errant strand of her light brown hair back from her forehead. "Of course I will, Jen," he answered, "if you want me to."

Turning out the lights, they walked upstairs together. Jenny was already beneath the covers when he switched off the bedside lamp and got in beside her, causing the old-fashioned bedsprings to shift beneath his weight.

Unlike the previous night, the shutters stood open. Moonlight flooded the room. A breeze stirred the pale, bunched mosquito netting, which was suspended from a ring near the ceiling and had been tied back to the bedposts.

"May I..." Jenny asked hesitantly.

Ned slipped one arm around her. "Be my guest."

For Jenny, nestling to sleep with her head on his shoulder was similar to being given a fortune she'd never expected to inherit. If I'm lucky, she thought, a pattern will be established. Maybe once the baby's born, something will come of it. We'll do more than share the same space. Though at the moment his willingness to be close to her was protective, not passionate, it gave her hope.

The following day, Arabella returned, bringing her four-year-old nephew, Napoleon, whose home had been devastated by the storm. "You let him stay here with me for a week or two while his parents rebuild, yes, missus?" the housekeeper asked.

Jenny smiled at the sober, dark-skinned child. "Of course he's welcome," she said, pleased by the distraction Napoleon would provide now that she felt too ungainly to do much walking and Ned was so preoccupied.

She quickly learned that the boy had never been more than a mile or so away from his home in Micoud and was somewhat retiring around strangers. Occupied caring for the house and catching up on a backlog of work, Arabella had very little time for him. Jenny, on the other hand, had nothing but time. And she was genuinely fond of children.

Taking Napoleon under her wing, she began reading to him from the illustrated storybooks left behind by Ned and his siblings on their St. Lucia vacations many years before. It was clear to her at once from his bashful comments and questions that he was quite intelligent. Yet he'd never been given pencil and paper to play with. Or learned anything of the alphabet.

The elementary-school teacher in her couldn't resist the challenge. "How would you like to learn your letters, Napoleon?" she asked the following afternoon as they sat side by side on the porch swing, watching a thundershower sweep down the cove. "I could show you how to write your name, and draw some pretty pictures for your mother."

His dark eyes solemn though she sensed he'd already begun to trust her, Napoleon shyly nodded.

Her plans and their budding friendship were cut short the third morning of his visit when Jenny started down the stairs and suddenly felt as if the bottom had dropped out of her physical self. Whooshing down her legs, a gush of clear fluid puddled on the mahogany treads at her feet.

Dear God, she thought. I'm barely eight months along. And my water has broken. It's too *soon*. The baby isn't finished yet.

Forcing herself to remain calm, she held on to the handrail and tried to think. Though she felt decidedly odd, labor pains hadn't started yet. She guessed she could expect them at any moment. It looked as if her baby's birth would be premature. And that meant high risk.

"Arabella," she called, unable to keep the sliver of panic she felt from surfacing in her voice. "Please . . . find Mr. Ned right away."

At that moment, the compact, dark-haired man who'd spent the past four nights in Jenny's bed was supervising the demolition of the resort's storm-battered charcoal shack. A frown drawing his emphatic brows together, he was debating whether to replace the structure or establish ornamental plantings in its place. Maybe the resort guests would enjoy an outdoor barbecue.

All such thoughts left his head as his new manager, Brian Ladreau, came sprinting over from the hotel.

"What's wrong?" Ned asked, scenting trouble.

"Your wife's gone into labor. She's asking for you."

It was too early by at least four weeks. *What if they lost the baby?* Refusing to entertain such a dire possibility, Ned ran for the Jeep. The acrid scent of burned rubber hung in the air as he took off at top speed, rapping his vehicle's tires against the asphalt pavement.

Jenny had lowered herself to a sitting position on the stairs by the time Ned came barreling in through the front door. Her pains had started and she was afraid to move. Vaguely sick to her stomach, she was still wearing her nightgown and robe.

"Jen...are you all right?" Ned asked, sitting down on the step below hers and taking both her hands in his. "Brian said you'd gone into labor."

Her green gaze blurred into his. "I think that's what's happening. Oh, Ned..."

She'd done nothing to cause a premature birth. She mustn't blame herself. Moving up a step, he put one arm around her. "I'm here, sweetheart," he said, the unpremeditated endearment slipping out as he drew her close. "Hang on to me. You can dig your nails into my arm if it helps."

"But...it's too early!"

He couldn't refute the point. Or deny that the situation worried him, too. "I know," he admitted. "We've got to get you to a hospital."

Just then, another of the oddly engrossing pains appeared. It seemed to originate in Jenny's pelvic area and rise to engulf her like a wave. She couldn't respond. As if she'd ceased to have a will of her own, she felt compelled to focus all her attention on it. Only when it had faded completely was she able to concentrate on him.

"That one was pretty strong," she whispered.

Totally lacking in experience where childbirth was concerned, Ned had blanched beneath his tan at the first hint of genuine suffering on Jenny's part. He didn't want her hurt, damn it! He'd rather bear the pain himself.

He doubted telling her so would help. "Eight minutes after nine," he observed soberly, glancing at the digital face of his watch. "As I understand it, we're supposed to time these things. Shall I help you to the living room before I call the doctor?''

If Ned thought it was all right for her to move, then Jenny would. Settling her amid a nest of pillows at one end of the couch, he strode to the phone. His eyes leaving her face just long enough to locate and dial the obstetrician's number, he demanded to be put straight through, whether or not Harry Cruikshank, M.D., was closeted with another patient.

After timing Jenny's pains over the phone, Dr. Cruikshank confirmed Ned's urge to get her to a hospital was right on target.

"If you have no objection, I'd prefer she deliver at Le Meynard, on Martinique," he said, naming the top medical facility on the neighboring island, which was a *département* of France. "I have staff privileges there. And they've got something we need...neonatal capability. At this stage of the game, the baby's birth weight's bound to be low. There could be complications. Tell you what...get your wife over to Vigie. I'll phone ahead for a charter flight and meet you at the airstrip."

Declining to pass the obstetrician's worries along to Jenny for obvious reasons, Ned barely gave Arabella time to pack her an overnight bag. But he was tenderness itself as he helped her to her feet.

"Do you think I should get dressed?" she asked doubtfully. "I don't feel much like it, to tell you the truth."

By their calculations, her pains were coming roughly a minute and a half apart. Ned doubted they had a great deal of time to waste. "Better not," he advised, anxious to deliver her into the hands of competent health-care professionals before things got out of control. "We don't want our son or daughter born en route to the delivery room."

Taking it step by step and leaning heavily on him, Jenny let Ned help her to the Jeep. She was about to get in when she paused, unable to do anything but focus as another pain gripped her. Each time one hit, it demanded her total concentration.

At last she sighed. "I guess we can go now."

Ned's brown eyes were anguished. "Was that a bad one?" he asked, settling her in the Jeep's passenger seat as if she were made of porcelain.

With a better idea of what to expect, Jenny wasn't frightened for herself—just concerned about her baby. "Not in the way you mean," she answered. "When I get a pain, I have to fit myself to it somehow. But the hurt isn't a *bad* hurt. It's more of a positive thing."

Ned didn't have the slightest idea what she was talking about. His own needs and desires in the situation were simple. He wanted the baby to be safe. And Jenny to have an easy time of it. He longed to protect them both with a ferocity that surprised him with its strength.

How could Milo have done this to her? he raged, wishing he could punch his irresponsible sibling in the face as he got in behind the wheel and turned his key in the ignition. She's suffering as a direct result of his selfishness. I'll never forgive him for running out on her the way he did.

Yet in a way he supposed he ought to thank his brother. If Milo hadn't been so lacking in ethics, he, Ned, wouldn't find himself at the brink of fatherhood. Instead, he'd probably still be trapped in the pattern of overwork and isolation he'd adopted as a result of Ronnie's betrayal.

I could never go back to living that way, he thought with sudden insight. Not in a million years. Meanwhile, though Jenny's discomfort tore at his heart, childbirth was a natural process. Soon it would be over. They'd be holding her baby in their arms.

Maybe *too* soon.

Though it might be his imagination, Jenny's pains seemed to be getting closer together. Nervous at the thought of presiding over the delivery himself, Ned leaned a little harder on the gas pedal as they streaked through the resort gates and made a sharp right at the bottom of the hill toward the huge piers where Balfour Shipping's banana boats docked.

As they crossed the little river bridge into downtown Castries, they picked up a police escort. Pointing to Jenny's stomach, Ned mouthed the words "Vigie," and "hospital." His overhead flashers continuing to operate, the policeman grinned and waved at them to follow him.

Ten minutes later they were aloft, rising above the sprawling city and its sun-silvered harbor, banking toward the north. The day was ideal, the iridescent blue waters of St. Lucia Channel crosshatched with diamonds. They could see famous La Diamant rock off the Martinique coast.

Accustomed to transporting patients between the two islands, the charter pilot and his manager had made Jenny as comfortable as possible on a collapsible gurney. As matter-of-factly as if they were in his Castries examining room, Dr. Cruikshank took her blood pressure and listened to her baby's heartbeat through his stethoscope. Though he nodded several times in apparent satisfaction, he didn't speak.

"Well?" Ned demanded irritably when at last the stethoscope dangled from its earpiece around his neck.

The obstetrician threw him an amused look. "Mother and baby doing fine. Father questionable."

Catching her breath between pains, Jenny let her mind drift. Ned was by her side, his fingers laced tightly through hers. And, though he'd suggested the trip to Fort de France because its hospital had special facilities, Dr. Cruikshank didn't seem all that worried. She began to believe everything would work out for the best.

In a way, she supposed, the birth of a child was similar to a force of nature. It sought its own rhyme and season, similar to birds responding to the instinct to migrate. Once it was underway, you might as well try to stop the ocean. As another pain lifted, she tried to relax and cooperate. The thrumming of the plane's twin engines wove itself into her physical sensations and her thoughts.

Their pilot had radioed ahead for an ambulance. Rushed to the hospital that was their destination within minutes after landing at Lamentin Airport, Jenny was taken directly to the labor room. With regret she assumed Ned would remain in some kind of waiting area, doing whatever it was expectant fathers did while their wives got on with the business at hand.

To her surprise, as soon as she was settled, he joined her. In place of the slacks and polo shirt he'd been wearing a few minutes earlier, he'd donned wrinkled green operating-room scrubs. With his frown of concern and take-charge manner, he could easily have passed for a surgeon.

"What's...this?" she managed to say, easing off a pain that had been her strongest yet.

Ned's voice was brisk, a little rough-edged. "You didn't think I'd leave you in the lurch, did you, Jen?"

Gazing at him, she thought of the stranger she'd bearded in his London office five months earlier. Blunt, skeptical, with a penchant for asking difficult questions, he'd seemed anything but husband material despite his undeniable sex appeal. Now she knew better. If someday he saw fit to return her love, she'd consider herself the luckiest woman on earth.

Her mouth curved despite the need to concentrate. "No," she said. "No, I didn't."

"Good. Because I'm here for the duration. We're in this thing together."

Handing Ned a damp cloth so he could wipe away the beads of sweat that were beginning to appear on Jenny's forehead, the labor-room supervisor, a middle-aged nurse with a decided French accent, explained how to coach her breathing. "Whether or not your wife 'as taken special classes," she said, "breathing correctly will 'elp."

Following her instructions to the letter while doing what he could to reassure and motivate Jenny, Ned was helpless to ease her pain very much. If Milo walked in the door right now, he thought again, I'd probably murder him. And again he acknowledged how much of the anger he'd felt toward his brother had dissipated.

In any real sense, Milo had ceased to matter vis à vis the drama of new life that was unfolding. Since Ned's marriage to Jenny, the small but precious being that had grown to the maturity of birth beneath her heart had belonged to him. That's true now emotionally as well as legally, he thought.

He wondered if Jenny felt as he did. Or was their bargain still a compromise she'd been forced to make in order to keep her baby? Such topics had been tacitly off limits, and he could do little more than guess. It comforted him to recall that she'd referred to her unborn infant as *ours* on a number of occasions. And, aside from their recent discussion of a long-ago Balfour family vacation during the hurricane, neither of them had mentioned Milo's name in the house for months.

Only time would tell. In the interim, after driving himself half-crazy with worry that the baby would be born before they reached the hospital, he'd begun to feel as if Jenny's labor would never end. It's taking so *long,* he agonized each time Dr. Cruikshank popped in, coffee cup in hand, or the middle-aged French nurse checked Jenny's progress and gently shook her head. Surely that's not typical. How much can she and the baby take?

In fact, Jenny's confinement was proceeding at a fairly rapid pace. Two hours after they'd reached the portals of Le Meynard, she was pronounced ready for the delivery room.

Despite Dr. Cruikshank's warning that the scene might be more graphic than he could stomach, Ned insisted on accompanying her. A mask covering his nose and mouth, he stood just behind her head, continuing to mop her brow as she gripped his free hand for all she was worth.

By now, Jenny's pains were overwhelming, encompassing the totality of her being. They flowed into one another almost without a break. Yet instinctively she guessed her ordeal would soon be over.

Seconds later, Dr. Cruikshank confirmed her assessment. "The baby's head is crowning," he said with an excitement that belied the many deliveries he'd attended. "Keep it up, Mrs. Balfour. You're doing wonderfully well. With your next pain, I want you to bear down as hard as you can...."

Jenny had just seconds to exchange a glance with Ned before her next pain arrived. Abandoning any urge she might have felt to husband her strength, she poured every ounce of energy and determination she possessed into an all-out effort to expel the baby.

"Again!" Dr. Cruikshank urged.

Jenny complied, barely pausing for breath. A momentary sense of relief was followed by renewed, almost unbearable pressure. Grimacing, she pushed even harder. She could feel the veins standing out at her temples as if they would burst.

Suddenly the baby's head and shoulders were free. With a spurt of ease, its lower body and feet emerged. They had a boy. Slippery, red and traumatized by his journey through the birth canal, he gasped at the first intrusion of air into his lungs. Seconds later, his quavery, thoroughly outraged newborn wail filled the delivery room.

Tears streamed unchecked down the hard planes of Ned's cheeks as Dr. Cruikshank examined the baby, logged his weight at five pounds and ten ounces and handed him to a nurse to be cleaned and wrapped in a blue receiving blanket. A few months shy of his fortieth birthday, Ned was a father. One day soon he'd hold out his hands to a chubby toddler and cushion his first steps. Teach his little son to play rugby in the park at Longwood. When the boy was a teenager, they'd sail the English Channel together.

Blinking from the drops that had been put in his eyes, the baby was placed in Ned's arms. As she watched him cradle the scrap of humanity that had come forth from her body, Jenny was crying softly, too. She loved them both so much.

"You see?" she said from the depths of her exhaustion and happiness as Ned smiled awkwardly at her through his tears. "It *was* Andrew from the beginning . . . a life for a life, the way you said."

Chapter Nine

" 'ave a 'appy life, *mes enfants*... all three of you!"
maternity-ward nurse Bernadette Leclerc called after
them when, five days later, Ned bundled his wife and
baby son into a taxi for their trip to Lamentin Airport.

For Jenny, the words were as much advice as bless-
ing. As she suckled Andrew during their brief flight
back to St. Lucia so he'd swallow and the altitude
wouldn't bother his ears, she vowed to do everything
she could to bring that blissful state of being about.

From an emotional standpoint, she knew, it would
involve a certain amount of risk-taking on her part.
Though Ned was clearly wild about the baby, easing
any fears she might have had that he'd hold Milo's role
in his conception against him, she didn't have the
slightest idea how her dark-haired husband felt about
her.

She could say with confidence that they were friends. Weathering a hurricane together had seen to that, as had sharing Andrew's birth. Yet when it came to forging a deeper, more intimate connection, she didn't have a scrap of evidence. Though the dark eyes that watched Andrew nuzzle at her engorged breast didn't attempt to hide their fascination, they were as enigmatic as ever when he raised them to her face. Ned Balfour the man, whom she guessed could please a woman to distraction, was still frustratingly out of reach.

When they reached the house, a congratulatory wire from Oliver and Viv was waiting for them on the hall table. In it, Ned's father and stepmother referred to the baby's fuzz of dark hair and expressed their opinion that the child looked like Ned.

"He does, rather," the latter observed with obvious satisfaction, chucking Andrew under the chin as Jenny prepared to put him down for a nap.

"You're right," she acknowledged, gently placing the baby in his cradle and tucking a light blanket around him. "How did they know? Did you describe Andrew to them in detail over the phone?"

With a shrug, Ned admitted he'd faxed the senior Balfours several photos he'd taken of the baby less than twenty-four hours after his birth. "Can I help it if I'm a disgustingly proud father?" he asked.

The telegram went on to address the matter of Andrew's christening, which Oliver emphasized ought to be held in England. "Trust you'll be home by Christmas," he'd concluded. "Best not to leave it too long."

"We have a lot to talk about," Ned observed. "Our return date, for one thing. And there's the matter of godparents. As I mentioned before, we'll need a larger, more permanent residence . . ."

His exuberant flow of plans came screeching to a halt when a second telegram arrived. "It's from Milo," he announced, scowling as he tipped the delivery boy and returned to the porch where he and Jenny had been having a late lunch.

Afraid whatever response she might make would strike a wrong note, Jenny hesitated. "What did he say?" she asked finally, aware that even a lack of interest on her part might be misinterpreted.

"That he wishes us the best. Here . . . read it for yourself."

Jenny wanted nothing to do with Milo or his sudden generosity. Neither did she wish to cause a scene. Reluctantly accepting the telegram, she scanned it and set it aside without comment. She didn't object, nor did Ned, when Arabella cleared the table and tossed it out with the garbage.

To her relief, Ned recovered from his annoyance sufficiently to remain home from work for the rest of the afternoon. Just looking at Andrew appeared to coax a better mood from him. He couldn't seem to get enough of watching her with the baby.

If only his enthusiasm would extend to continuing the sleeping arrangement we began just prior to Andrew's birth, she thought as they rocked on the porch that evening and Ned offered the baby a blunt, powerful index finger to grasp. Once I've recovered from the birth, I'd stand a better chance with him.

At last it was time for bed. Ned offered to carry the baby upstairs. After kissing Andrew's cheek and laying him in his cradle, he wished Jenny good-night.

He was about to go. Summoning her courage, she detained him with a light touch.

"Stay," she whispered. "That is, I don't mind if you'd prefer to sleep here, in order to be close to the baby."

If she was blushing, Ned wasn't aware of it. Overwhelmed by a sudden urge to do exactly what she was suggesting, he considered the situation. It had been more than a year since he'd made love to a woman and his body ached for it. Now that Jenny was no longer pregnant, he'd find it difficult to maintain their platonic relationship if he shared her bed.

They'd promised each other a marriage-in-name-only, one not honeycombed with the pitfalls of jealousy and devotion. If at some point she wanted to scrap the rules, that didn't mean he did.

A moment later he decided he was imagining things. Jenny wasn't propositioning him. She wasn't in any *shape* for a man. He'd seen firsthand what childbirth could do, and he was well aware her body needed to heal. She also needed rest. From what he knew of infants, they woke up in the middle of the night, demanding to be fed. For several weeks, at least, she'd be on call around the clock.

"You'll sleep better without me, Jen," he decided, his dark gaze sliding away from hers. "If you need me for anything, I'll be in the next room."

Shamelessly she stood her ground. "Kiss me goodnight, then."

In a phone conversation with Ned that morning, Jenny's obstetrician had warned that her moods might fluctuate. He'd spoken of postpartum depression. Apparently the problem had something to do with hormones.

She needs reassurance, that's all, he told himself. If only she didn't look so fetching in that nightgown, with her hair loose around her shoulders.

"Of course I will, if you like," he said.

The light brush of his lips against her forehead only exacerbated Jenny's longing to feel close to him. I can't stand this wall between us, she thought. I want to tear it down with my hands.

Action following impulse, she returned the kiss with one of her own on his mouth.

Despite everything they'd been through together, it was their first. Though Ned flinched, his response was immediate. Her softly parted lips and the voluptuous invitation of her body caused him to be aroused in an instant.

She was in no condition for a loving onslaught. And he'd vowed never to take advantage of her. If he did so now—capitalizing on the emotional insecurity her physician had said could result from childbirth—he'd never forgive himself.

"Jen, this is wrong," he said, pulling back. "I'm not going to use you this way."

In a furor to hide the evidence of his arousal, he bade her a hasty good-night. He didn't see the film of tears his words evoked.

By morning, Ned had survived his embarrassment. But not the impulsive kiss that had made him desire Jenny so much. Confused, his defenses threatened by his strong attraction to her, he was grateful when she didn't mention it. Or even act as if it had occurred.

Life would have been exceedingly uncomfortable for him if she had. As she and Andrew settled into a placid routine, he couldn't seem to stay away. Despite everything he had to do, supervising the rest of the hurricane cleanup and final preparations for the resort's grand opening, he came home every day for lunch. Whenever possible, he knocked off early to be with them.

From what Jenny could tell, nothing pleased him better than watching her nurse the baby. It's as if he's never seen a woman suckle an infant before, she thought, and regards it as some kind of miracle. Maybe that's because his first wife would never have given herself so freely to anything of the sort.

For perhaps the hundredth time, she asked herself if the first Mrs. Balfour's refusal to have children could possibly explain Ned's willingness to enter into a marriage without sex or romantic commitment. She had to conclude it didn't. As the days passed and he continued to behave like a devoted husband in every way but one, she wondered if she'd ever know the truth.

They were halcyon days in every other respect. When Andrew was too weeks old, Ned began taking them for short drives around the property. Clearly he loved to show the baby off and soon everyone was *oohing* and *aahing* over him. When Howie Chappell dropped by for a visit and remarked that he'd never thought he'd see Ned's Jeep sporting an infant car seat, Jenny took it as an accolade.

Only one thing was needed to make her life complete. A month after Andrew's birth, when Dr. Cruikshank mentioned it would be all right for her to resume marital relations, she decided to give fate a push.

The resort's grand opening was just a few weeks away. Desperate for some new clothes now that she had a waistline again, Jenny left Andrew in Arabella's care one jewel-bright afternoon and took a taxi into Castries to remedy the situation.

Recommended by the housekeeper, who had a large coterie of gentlemen friends along with some stunning party dresses, the couturiere she sought maintained a tiny, second-floor atelier on tree-shaded Columbus Square, near Rain Restaurant and the Roman Catholic cathedral. Though the stairs that led up from a faded placard at street level were anything but promising, Jenny knew she'd come to the right place when she saw the sari-clad tradeswoman's gorgeous stock of fabric.

Introducing herself as Mrs. Gupta and bidding Jenny a polite welcome, the dressmaker asked her to describe the sort of gown she wanted.

"Something for a party that will make my husband fall in love with me," Jenny answered truthfully.

Her mouth curving slightly as if Jenny had made a little joke, Mrs. Gupta positioned her in front of a three-way mirror. She didn't understand the situation, of course. Yet by instinct, perhaps, she seemed to envision exactly the kind of dress Jenny had in mind. The second bolt of fabric she held beneath Jenny's chin was a blue-green silk paved with sequins in the same color.

Oh, thought Jenny. *Yes.*

"It's good, I think?" Mrs. Gupta suggested.

Quickly executed, the dressmaker's sketch had Jenny convinced. To seduce Ned, she'd wear a modest, sleeveless, round-necked sheath that suited her personality yet followed her every curve like water and emphasized her newly slender waist. The matching chiffon stole the woman proposed as an afterthought would only add to the gown's demure yet unabashed sexiness.

Diffidently Mrs. Gupta named her price. To Jenny, who had a history of buying clothes on sale or at a discount, it sounded exorbitant. Yet she was convinced it would be worth every penny. Stifling her guilt, she wrote out a deposit and stood lost in daydreams as the dressmaker took her measurements.

After several fittings, Jenny's wonderful dress was ready to wear. It hung swathed in a dustcover at the back of her armoire, out of sight. She didn't want Ned to see it until the proper moment. Now and then she reached back to fondle it, as if to reassure herself of its presence.

During the weeks of its creation, Ned had completed the necessary storm repairs. His vision of the resort had been realized. On the Friday morning that marked the beginning of his long-awaited grandopening weekend, he stopped by Jenny's room for a brief word before plunging into the day's round of activities.

Dressed in a loose, pin-tucked nightgown he remembered from her pregnancy, she was lounging in one of the window seats, nursing the baby. Her slim, tanned legs dangled coltishly to the floor. Of necessity, one side of her bodice hung open, the nipple thus bared concealed by Andrew's mouth.

Glancing up at his approach, she gave him an affectionate smile. He looked so sexy and powerful in his tropical-weight suit. "Good luck," she said. "I'm sure everything will be fabulous."

She was the same woman he'd sheltered during a hurricane and coached through childbirth. And yet she wasn't. In the dowdy nightgown, with her hair mussed from sleep and her face bare of makeup, she was part Madonna. Yet she managed to call forth a stab of longing so intense he felt as if a truck had slammed into his gut.

"Is anything wrong?" she added with a puzzled expression when he didn't speak. "You look so preoccupied."

With effort, Ned got a grip on himself. "Sorry," he answered. "My head's full of details, I guess. I've got to run. Don't forget... tonight's party night. Remind Arabella of her promise to baby-sit."

Throughout the long morning and afternoon, Jenny watched from her hilltop perch as the resort's first guests arrived. Though it was early December, the weather was gorgeous. The welcome party Ned had mentioned had been planned for the pool area outside the restaurant. They'd asked Arabella to baby-sit so Jenny could attend.

For once, despite the help of Brian Ladreau, who would assume full responsibility in a few weeks when they returned to England, Ned was too busy to come home and check on his wife and son during the lunch hour. Around 6:00 p.m., still unable to break away though he'd planned to come for Jenny in the Jeep, he phoned to ask if she'd mind driving over with Brian's wife after she finished feeding the baby.

His enforced preoccupation meshed perfectly with her plans. From the moment she'd ordered her dress, she'd imagined herself springing it on him in a public place and now she'd be able to carry out that fantasy.

Handing the baby to Arabella to rock when he was sated with milk, she hurried upstairs to bathe and change. First came a shower. Then makeup. Ordering herself not to hurry, she slipped into bikini panties and a garter belt, whisper-sheer hose. Because of her nursing state, Mrs. Gupta had fashioned her gown with a built-in bra and special leak-proof lining. Naked to the waist, Jenny slipped it over her head.

Silken next to her skin, it seemed almost to pour over her curves. Not yet, she thought, postponing her first glimpse as she pulled up its zipper tab. First I want to put on the matching shoes and my crystal drop earrings... get the full effect.

At last she was ready as she'd ever be. Chills ran down her spine as she regarded herself in the oval, full-length mirror that stood in one corner of her room. The transformation from charity case and expectant mother was complete. On impulse, she shook her hair free of its usual Edwardian knot, letting it float sensuously around her shoulders.

Her heart was in her throat as she and Cecie Ladreau arrived at the restaurant-pool complex where the party was already underway. What if Ned rejects me? she thought. Or doesn't even notice the result of my efforts?

Parking Cecie's Fiat in a loading zone above and behind the restaurant kitchen, they started down the curving stone steps that led to the patio and pool area. As Jenny paused with the manager's wife just behind her to scan the crowd, the scene was straight out of a travel brochure—lighted free-form pool, reggae band, swaying palm trees.

A sumptuous buffet had been set up under white Japanese umbrellas. Cocktail glasses clinked. People laughed. Some of them were dancing. The *hush-hush* of surf that broke on the beach below wove itself into the music like an aphrodisiac.

Moments later, she spotted her husband. Having dispatched one of the hotel porters to the house to fetch his evening clothes, he'd showered and changed into them at his office. His untamed, predatory quality contrasting sharply with the glamour and sophistication of a formal bow tie and dinner jacket, he was the most attractive man in sight.

Gesturing to make a point with the strong, bluntly manicured hands that had been her lifeline during Andrew's birth, he was conversing with a group of wealthy-looking visitors she guessed included several cruise-line executives. One of the women, a stunning blonde in a white spandex mini that emphasized the curve of her buttocks, was flirting openly with him.

Ned chose that exact moment to look up. And caught his breath. *Jenny* had arrived. In her shimmery dress she looked like a mermaid dripping jeweled Caribbean droplets. Abruptly the fragmented, fuzzy, imperfectly realized feelings that had haunted him for weeks coalesced. He still couldn't name them. Murmuring what he hoped was a coherent excuse, he made his way through the crowd to meet her at the foot of the steps.

Her lips parting softly, she didn't speak.

"My God, Jen…you're exquisite," he growled, his hands settling possessively at her waist. "What on earth did you do to yourself?"

It wasn't a compliment in the traditional sense. But Jenny didn't mind. Ned had *definitely* noticed. The hungry, incredulous way he was staring at her was accolade enough.

From the beginning, she'd guessed Ned Balfour was like a great jungle cat in his sexuality. He'd just never offered her any personal evidence. Something in his past, apparently, had prompted him to keep that side of himself under wraps.

Now it was glowing in his deep brown eyes. He was standing so close she felt as if he were ready to devour her. The warmth of his breath was a sensual demand against her mouth.

It occurred to her that perhaps she ought to say something. "I dressed up for the party," she answered innocently. "That was the idea, wasn't it? Shouldn't you introduce me to some of the guests?"

That night, as they mingled and danced and celebrated the successful completion of his project, Ned was never far from her side. He couldn't get enough of touching her. Or drinking in the pheromone-laden molecules of her perfume.

As hosts, they had to stay until 10:00 p.m. But after that, he vowed, his new manager would be required to earn his keep. He and Jenny had some things to settle. As they moved together in the flower-scented moonlight, he was torn between the flame of his desire and a persistent, unanswered question.

At last the hour of their release arrived. "C'mon . . . let's get out of here," he whispered gruffly. "We have to talk."

Talk? thought Jenny in dismay as he settled her chiffon stole around her shoulders and led her up the steps to the Jeep. That's not what this is about!

She was somewhat heartened by the way he drew her close as he started the engine. Yet as her stole fluttered in the soft breeze and she leaned her head against the hard bulk of his shoulder, she couldn't forget the formal, off-putting way he'd thanked her for acting as his "hostess" after they'd danced together at Gros Islet. Or his unequivocal return to their previous sleeping arrangements after Andrew's birth. If he behaved that way again, she believed, the risk-taking woman in her would be crushed.

Arabella was waiting up for them. "The little one is fas' asleep," she announced with a smile. "I promise my boyfriend I will meet him after you get home, okay?"

Ned's strong features were a study in suppressed emotion. "Fine with us," he answered shortly, tugging Jenny toward the stairs.

They were alone in the house as they checked on Andrew. Though he'd be awake, whimpering to be fed in an hour or so, currently Arabella's status report was correct. He was lying on his tummy in the cradle Ned's employee had made for him, his diaper-padded bottom humped in the air.

"Sweet baby..."

Jenny's mermaid dress glittered in the moonlight as she leaned over to kiss her son, then stepped aside so Ned could say good-night to him. By now she knew he loved Andrew as much as she did. It didn't seem to matter to him that the child had been fathered by his brother.

With a featherweight delicacy that belied his strength, Ned stroked the baby's cheek. A moment later he was raising his eyes to hers.

"We have to talk," he reiterated.

He was about to reject her again.

"Oh, please..."

Turning away, she went to stand by the window. On the lawn below, moonlight splashed across the flower beds. Faint laughter drifted upward from the steps that led to the beach. It was a safe bet that Arabella and her gentleman friend wouldn't stand on ceremony.

Deterred by Jenny's sudden withdrawal from him, Ned wasn't quite sure how to proceed. All evening long, as they'd touched and entwined like lovers, she'd seemed to want what he wanted. Now she didn't. Had he completely misread her? If he confessed that he yearned for her past bearing, would she refuse him? Insist they keep their bargain to the letter?

He could think of only one way to find out. Crossing the room to stand behind her, he lifted her hair away from her neck, then let it fall.

"Back in May, when I outlined the kind of marriage I felt I could offer you," he began, his husky growl just inches from her ear, "I never dreamed we'd be living in such close proximity. I envisioned a polite, far more distant relationship...."

Shivery with arousal just seconds earlier from the light brush of his fingers, Jenny's neck and shoulders tensed. Dear God, she thought. Is he going to say he wants *more* distance between us?

Ned detected her increased rigidity at once. But he didn't know what to make of it. Though he'd long since stopped thinking she might be amoral or grasping, a daunting possibility continued to trouble him.

What if she still cared for his brother?

If she *was* carrying a torch for Milo, her sudden recoil made sense. And he was about to make an utter fool of himself. Desire so strong it was a physical ache in his gut wouldn't let him retreat. Neither would a more complex emotion he wasn't ready to put into words.

He decided to hedge his bets.

"What I neglected to consider when I outlined the terms of our marriage agreement was the fact that I'm a normal man, with basic desires and appetites," he said as offhandedly as he could, "just as you're a normal woman. Our sexual needs aren't likely to go unmet forever. In the interest of maintaining a stable marriage for Andrew's sake, wouldn't it make sense for us to meet them for each other?"

Chapter Ten

Usually so articulate, Ned had blurted out a pompous hopelessly distorted rendition of what he felt. To his chagrin, he'd made it sound as if anyone would have filled the bill, whereas he was eaten up with lust and longing for just one woman.

Meanwhile, though the night air was cool, Jenny's cheeks were burning. He's suggesting we serve as sexual lightning rods for each other! she thought in distress. Is this...this *parody* of loving to be the outcome of my fondest hopes?

When she didn't answer, Ned edged toward desperation. Maybe she *is* in love with Milo, he mentally flogged himself. Though it meant risking his self-esteem, he decided to put her to the test.

"Jen, if you don't want me, say so," he begged, taking hold of her zipper tab and slowly parting the glimmery fabric of her dress.

A moment later, he was feathering little kisses down her backbone. For Jenny, the sensation was electric. Stabbed to the quick with love for him and overcome by an erotic craving so deep she'd never known its equal, she turned to face him.

A confession was wrung from her lips.

"*I* want you..."

Seconds later they were mauling each other with kisses. Emboldened, Ned dragged her bodice to her waist. In return, she reached for his buttons. Soon his dinner jacket and shirt, her exquisite party dress were on the floor. Their fingers meeting awkwardly in their haste, they disposed of her nylons, panties and garter belt.

"You, too," Jenny insisted when she was fully naked in his arms.

Her unabashed desire had him hot in seconds. Unfastening his belt, Ned divested himself of his trousers. In his rush to dress for the evening's festivities, he hadn't bothered with underwear.

He was even bigger than she'd thought the day their eyes had met in the mirrors aboard his yacht. And so beautiful. Though her only previous experience with sex had been terrible—Milo's drunken theft of her virginity—she wanted to sheath Ned in her hands. Stroke and kiss him. Learn his entrancing shape.

His strong features blunted with passion, he couldn't get enough of touching her. As he caressed her sensitive peaks, instant communication opened between them and Jenny's most private places. Just by touching her, it seemed, Ned could cause her insides to open and ache for him.

Not pausing to consider how blatant the gesture might seem, she rubbed her upper body against his hair-roughened chest. Ned thrust against her, overcome by her frank sensuality. He longed to take her standing up, with her beautiful legs wrapped around him. Or on a swing. In a rocking chair. They had one in the living room....

"Jen?" he asked, his dark eyes narrow slits. "Do you want us in bed? Or..."

Her pupils widened. What did he have in mind? "I'm willing to try whatever you suggest," she whispered.

He wanted to please her before taking his own satisfaction. Though under the circumstances her experience was a given, something told him her encounters with men hadn't been all that numerous.

"Bed," he decided after a moment, deferring to gut-level instinct. "We'll close the mosquito curtains."

It was an inspired bit of stage-setting on his part. In a way he'd only dimly anticipated, drawing the milky-white, diaphanous curtains around Jenny's bed transformed it into the wedding bower they'd never shared.

Though Andrew was asleep nearby, attesting to her fruitfulness, in her magical, white-draped seclusion she looked almost virginal. In every way that counts, I'm a satyr about to deflower a maiden, Ned fantasized, letting her pull him into her arms. Yet a mortal man, sharing Aphrodite's bedchamber. Though his thoughts were less than coherent, they described exactly what he felt. He wanted Jenny shy but explicit, unopened flower *and* love goddess. To his amazement, she was both.

Covering her breasts and the surprisingly taut, flat mount of her stomach with kisses, he parted her legs to stroke her nest of light brown curls. She was moist and ready, rife with sexual perfume, and she shivered as he ventured deeper, seeking and finding the secret nub of her desire.

"Ned . . . oh, *Ned!*"

Overwhelmed by the heated response he'd evoked, she meshed her fingers in his thick, dark hair. She'd never been caressed that way. In his assault on her virtue, Milo hadn't given a moment's thought to pleasing her. Nor would she willingly have allowed him to be so intimate.

Now Ned was touching her. She wanted to give him everything, be his fine-tuned instrument. Without consciously deciding to, she let go of every handhold she knew. Spirals of sensation taking her, she bore down with the soles of her feet.

Inevitably she'd lose control. No sooner had Jenny recognized that fact than she felt herself slipping past the point of no return. Helpless, a prisoner of her mounting ecstasy, she hovered at the brink.

Seconds later, a feast of shudders claimed her, causing her to gasp in surprise. Abandoning herself to the feeling, she flushed with heat. Her thighs were suffused with the sweet ache of fulfillment.

I never dreamed it could be this way, she thought, tingling to the soles of her feet. *Never guessed there could be such bliss in loving.*

To Ned, her basic innocence was suddenly apparent. *No one has ever done this for her before,* he realized in amazement. *In that sense, she is a virgin.* Though she'd had sex with his brother for what he believed had been a period of weeks and possibly with other men while she was still in America, it had fallen to him to initiate her.

The idea fired his imagination. No neophyte himself, though he'd endured a long, dry spell, he burned to plunge into her to the hilt, plumb her deepest places. Not yet, he cautioned himself, attempting to curb his eagerness. Let her savor the moment.

For Jenny, her culmination had been like a little death. Slates had been wiped clean. All tension had drained from her body. She was becalmed now, floating in an isolation tank of contentment.

Paradoxically she was in close contact with the man she loved. "Ned, you haven't..." she whispered, opening her eyes as if she'd heard every word he thought.

"Hush. We have time, sweetheart. I want you to feel everything."

"I am. Oh, I am. But if the baby wakes..."

"Then we'll wait until you've finished feeding him."

"I want you now."

Refusing to take *no* for an answer, she reached for him. Lovingly she stroked his manhood, smoothing each ridge and detail with her fingertips.

Ned's groan was an admission of helplessness. "You know I can't hold out against you...."

A moment later he was fitting himself to her, probing the moist, deep refuge between her legs. God, but she's wonderful, he thought, holding them briefly motionless. So tight and ready for me though the baby isn't quite two months old.

Thinking of Andrew made him realize he hadn't provided them with birth control. "Jen, we can't," he confessed in anguish, starting to withdraw from her. "You'll get pregnant again. I didn't..."

Clasping Ned's buttocks with her feet, she wouldn't let him go. "I did," she confessed. "Dr. Cruikshank and I took care of things when I went in for my checkup."

She'd been planning this for several weeks.

At the discovery, his desire for her was limitless. "You mean...you're safe?" he asked, his voice so nasal with passion it was almost unrecognizable.

She nodded.

He thrust deeper, his satyr's madness gathering. "I won't be able to last."

In response, she lifted her lower body from the bed to meet him. "It's okay," she whispered, glowing at the way he looked, moving in and out of her. "We have all night."

His face a mask of need above hers, Ned drove to fulfillment. Moments before he cried out in his rapture, Jenny thought she might make the trip again. As shudders of gooseflesh spread over his skin, she guessed it would have been different—more soul-shattering than her first experience, and incredibly deep.

To their surprise, Andrew didn't wake. Lying sated beside her, with one knee thrust between her thighs, Ned traced a line from her feminine mysteries to her chin, with detours to her nipples. He finished with a blunt little caress of her parted lips.

"You almost got there again, didn't you?" he asked.

Suddenly shy, she nodded. Was she too much of a wanton for his taste?

He quieted her fears before she could draw another breath. "I don't know about you," he drawled with a touch of the wry self-mockery she found so appealing, "but I'll be ready again in twenty minutes. The way I feel, I could keep you awake all night."

Shortly after 3:00 a.m. Jenny woke to her son's plaintive whimpering. She and Ned were sprawled on her bed atop tangled sheets. In the interim, they'd made love twice more. Both times he'd taken her all the way with him. Afterward he'd pulled up a light coverlet.

His face turned toward her in sleep, he'd laid one hand on her breast in a proprietary gesture. A beam of moonlight surprised an almost boyish look on his face.

How I love him! she thought. More every moment. She prayed he wouldn't back off, dismiss the wonder of what they'd shared.

Reluctantly detaching herself from his embrace, she slipped on a robe and took the baby to the window seat. Her dress and Ned's evening clothes lay scattered where they'd dropped them. As she offered Andrew her breast, she immersed herself in the memories of what had taken place.

Once the barriers were down, they'd done more loving than talking. She could think of nothing Ned had said to negate his preposterous suggestion that they make love to each other out of sexual convenience. He'd made no mention of that singular commodity called "love." She doubted it was what he felt.

Yet she hadn't given up hope. She had a lot to be thankful for. Something more tender than lust had been present in his concern for her pleasure. Unless she was kidding herself, she'd felt it in his caresses, too, and the way he'd sheltered her as they went to sleep.

When at last she put her son back in his cradle and returned to bed, Ned didn't wake. Accommodating her as if they'd slept together for years, he curled around her so that they fitted against each other like spoons. She drifted back to sleep with her rump securely cradled by his thighs and one muscular, faintly hirsute arm wrapped around her waist.

In the morning, she woke late. The sun was up, a breeze stirring her filmy bed curtains. Only the disheveled condition of her sheets and the delicious ache that had settled into her muscles testified to the fact that she and Ned were lovers who'd spent the night together.

He'd left no note—simply washed, dressed and slipped out of the house while she was still asleep. By now, he was almost certainly immersed in the business of his grand opening, his mind light years removed from her.

As she picked up Andrew to give him his morning bath, she couldn't help but wonder if her ardent lover of the nighttime hours was having second thoughts. A few minutes later, as she was washing behind the baby's perfect, shell-shaped ears and speaking love words to him, she remembered Ned had chartered the *Brig Unicorn,* a one hundred and forty-foot, square-rigged sailing ship used mostly for tourist excursions, to transport a group of his VIPs down St. Lucia's west coast. They'd view the Pitons up close, visit the semiactive "drive-in" volcano and nearby rain forest, sightsee in the unspoiled coastal town of Soufrière.

Ned, she knew, would be hosting the trip. In the crush of activity preceding the grand opening, he hadn't mentioned the possibility that she might accompany him. Probably that's because I can't be separated from the baby for very long, she decided.

She doubted he remembered the promise he'd made that day on the Morne, while she was still pregnant, to take her by boat to see the island's most dramatic mountains. Or that the opportunity would present itself again before they left for London.

The phone rang and, with Andrew half closed in a clean diaper, she let Arabella pick it up in the kitchen. Apparently it wasn't for her. Responding a few times, the housekeeper hung up. Though Jenny's hopes had soared, she supposed that, under the circumstances, a call from Ned was too much to expect. Cuddling Andrew against her shoulder, she started downstairs to feed him his baby cereal.

Arabella met her at the landing. "Mr. Ned jus' phoned," she said, her eyes dancing with excitement. "He wants you, Andrew an' me to go along on this morning's boat trip. He say, 'tell Mrs. Jen to get a move on!'"

Assigning Arabella to feed Andrew his cereal and pack the diaper bag with every conceivable necessity for a day's outing, Jenny raced back upstairs. She was so ecstatic her feet felt as if they barely touched the treads. He wants me with him! she exulted, jumping in the shower and turning on the water full blast.

She dressed for the trip in a striped T-shirt with a boat neck and push-up sleeves, and white cotton shorts. In lieu of underwear she wore a miniscule, fire-engine-red bikini she'd bought the day she'd ordered her mermaid dress.

Though the suit fit her perfectly and was amazingly flattering to her curves, she hadn't worked up the courage to wear it in public yet. Now she'd take the plunge. If they swam off the boat as she'd heard tourists often did, she wanted to tantalize Ned.

Arabella had dressed Andrew in a sailor suit. Apparently having caught the housekeeper's mood, he was cooing and waving his bootie-clad feet in the air.

"My precious little man," Jenny enthused, picking him up and hugging him. "You're so handsome... just like your daddy, Ned."

Just then the Jeep's horn sounded. With Andrew in tow, she and Arabella rushed out the door. The man who'd pleased Jenny so immoderately the night before gave her a wry, appreciative look as he settled them in their seats.

"You didn't think I'd forget my promise, did you?" he asked as he threw the Jeep into gear.

And then he laughed. Obviously she had. As they breezed past the resort gates, he reached over and captured her hand.

"You should have known better," he reproved with mock severity. "In your defense, you probably aren't awake yet. I understand you slept rather late."

They were the last passengers to board the big, lively looking schooner before its crew cast off. As it chugged away from the dock under auxiliary power, nosing out into Castries Harbor with its stunning views of the city, Vigie peninsula and Balfour Beach, the sails filled up with breeze. It was life from a completely different perspective.

With Andrew safely ensconced in Arabella's lap and Ned beside her at the rail, Jenny thought she'd never known such bliss. In his khaki shorts and open-necked cotton shirt, with the wind disarranging his hair, Ned looked exactly like the tanned, fit, somewhat guarded executive who'd met her at Vigie Airport when she'd arrived from London nearly six months earlier. But he wasn't—not to her. Their night together had changed them both. They were lovers now, the keepers of each other's passionate secrets.

Between them, the slightest touch telegraphed intimacy, passionate moments to come. Jenny's comfort zone kept expanding. It deepened perceptibly as he draped one arm around her shoulders.

As they passed the point where Ned had all but finished construction of what would be Balfour Beach's most expensive villas, the breeze was heavenly. It was heaven just to be alive. Even the next cove south, home of the industrialized Hess Oil complex, fascinated her.

In the distance, the first of St. Lucia's rugged mountain peaks appeared, dissolving silver green in cloud cover. Marigot Bay—hurricane hole, movie site and port of call to the international yachting community—came next, then the mouth of Roseau Valley, spilling a flood of banana plantations toward turquoise shallows and creaming breakers. Beneath the *Unicorn*'s hull, the water was foam-flecked, the color of dark blue ink. Coconut palms rode the humping green hills like sentinels.

They passed several villages where fishing boats had been beached on the sugary brown sand. Rusting tin roofs shone red and silver as they caught the sunlight. The boxlike houses that straggled up the hills from ramshackle jetties were every color of the rainbow.

"There you are, Jen," Ned said as they passed a vine-clad headland. "Your much vaunted Pitons."

Basking in his casual but affectionate tone, which hinted he was offering them to her as a kind of gift, she leaned over the rail. Just beyond the bulk of Mount Gimie were the steep, conical peaks she'd longed to see at close range.

Emblematic of the island, the Pitons were a centuries old landfall for Caribbean sailors. "They're

wonderful!'' she exclaimed, resisting the urge to spoil
her unspoken communication with her husband by
putting her gratitude into words. "The kind of sight
that, when you first see it, gives you a shivery little
sensation in the pit of your stomach."

Ned's Bogart brows lifted slightly. "A thoroughly
feminine description, if I may say so," he teased. "To
a man, they resemble a splendiferous pair of breasts."

For Jenny's sake, he'd asked the *Unicorn*'s captain
to sail to the very foot of the spectacular twin peaks
known as Gros Piton and Petit Piton, which rose precipitously from the sea's iridescent depths with no
beach in sight. Afterward, they backtracked and
docked at the blue-turquoise-and-cream-colored
nineteenth-century town of Soufrière—a traditional
tour stop with its French colonial buildings and ami-
able population.

A fleet of taxi vans was waiting for them. With
Arabella riding beside them and Andrew on Jenny's
lap, they drove up steep, jungle-clad hills Ned said received more than one hundred and fifty inches of
rainfall a year to view the volcano's muddy, bubbling, sulphur-scented crater. As arranged, a guide
recited its history and noted that its temperature was
three hundred and eighty degrees Fahrenheit beneath
the surface. She also pointed out various exotic plantings, including a number of orchids. For the first time,
Jenny saw cashew nuts growing as if an afterthought
at the bottom of odd-looking, puckery fruits.

Everyone was hungry by the time they returned to
the boat. With that likelihood in mind, a buffet had
been set up featuring island curry and various local
delicacies such as stuffed breadfruit and mango ice

cream. While Jenny nursed Andrew, Ned placed alternate bites of curry into her mouth.

Relaxing atop the schooner's cabin, with their backs against the forward mast, they were in full public view. And, despite his willingness to shock on occasion, she'd never have called Ned an exhibitionist. Yet with a subtlety that had them both tingling all over, he managed to make feeding her seem an erotic exercise.

A short time later, the baby was asleep in Arabella's arms and they were anchoring off an unnamed stretch of shoreline for a swim. Stripping to their suits, Ned and Jenny prepared to join the crowd of revelers who were already splashing alongside the boat.

Her red bikini was a definite hit. Ned looked her over from head to toe. "If you don't mind my saying so," he deadpanned, breast-shaped mountains the farthest thing from his head, "that suit's rather too modest. Couldn't you have found something a bit more titillating?"

Jenny's eyes glinted with satisfaction at the backhanded compliment. *She'd* been comparing the rippling muscles of his torso to those of Michelangelo's *David*. Of course, Ned was much more mature than the boy who'd posed for the famous Renaissance sculpture. And far sexier, in her opinion.

"Why don't we discuss it in the water?" she asked, diving off the top of the ladder without waiting for him.

With several seconds' head start, she managed to stay ahead of him for a few strokes. But only a few. As she'd hoped, he caught up with her almost at once. Snaring her in his powerful arms, he dragged her beneath the crystal-clear water.

Because of treacherous currents, the *Unicorn* had anchored some distance offshore and the water was fairly deep. Down, down they went, her thighs gripping his waist. If we had gills, we could make love right here, Jenny fantasized as they kissed hungrily and deeply, with his tongue in her mouth. Insinuating herself against him, she longed to feel his hardness and heat deep within her body.

They were still mouth-to-mouth as they broke the surface. Laughter took over at once. "Round two," Ned warned, pulling her back down and raining erotic kisses on her navel.

Tenderness, not deviltry, was uppermost as he wrapped her in an oversize beach towel by the *Unicorn*'s rail. Yet as they started back to Castries so the resort guests could rest and recuperate for the cocktail hour, Jenny guessed, the same thing was on both their minds.

So close in a physical sense it seemed they could almost inhabit the same skin, they couldn't wait to get their hands on each other. The reasoning that propelled him into my arms doesn't matter, Jenny decided as she leaned her head against his shoulder. Just the fact that he's finally there. Maybe if I'm patient, someday he'll return the strong love I feel for him.

They drove straight home from the dock. Giving Arabella the rest of the day off, Ned took Andrew from her and carried him upstairs. "I'll watch him so you can have a shower, if you like," he told Jenny in a matter-of-fact tone.

She *did* want to get the salt water off her skin and perfume her body before she nestled in his arms. Pausing to watch a moment as he plopped down on their rumpled bed and positioned Andrew on his chest, Jenny thought how utterly sexy he was. And how gentle with the baby.

He wants to prolong the waiting...make us half-wild with it, she realized. Just as he wanted to get Arabella out of the house so we don't have to be circumspect.

Leaning over to kiss their son, she disappeared into her private bathroom to luxuriate in warm, soapy water and think of Ned. When she returned, wrapped in a towel with one end tucked between her breasts, Andrew was asleep, burrowed against the chest of the man who'd volunteered to be his father.

Ned watched as she transferred the baby to his cradle. "Come here," he said thickly as she turned to face him.

While she'd been putting the baby down, he'd taken off his swimming trunks. Dropping her towel without breaking eye contact, she got into bed with him. Sunlight was streaming in through the windows. They'd be able to see every grimace of pleasure, every telltale goose bump.

Moving astride him, Jenny kissed him with parted lips. He responded by rubbing himself against her. Within seconds, they were scaling the footholds to paradise.

Chapter Eleven

Obsessed with each other, Ned and Jenny continued to explore their newfound intimacy as the holidays approached. They made love on the porch swing—drunkenly, though they'd imbibed no alcohol. In an armless rocker in the living room, all but wearing a groove in the floor. They even coupled on the beach one moonless night while Arabella baby-sat, their hunger enhanced by the threat of discovery as they ravished each other.

Yet her antique four-poster was their most frequent recourse. Within its feather-bedded nest and the sanctuary of her breeze-swept room, they strung erotic encounters together like love beads. Separate instances of laughter, lovemaking, sleeping together beneath the same bed covers and waking to renew their deepening involvement merged in a seamless ambience that was both reassuring and profoundly sensual.

Whenever they touched in public, whether by accident or design, shared knowledge of their private moments flickered between them. Yet not a single love word was exchanged. Certain an emotional wound or disappointment he didn't want to talk about had caused Ned to throw up fortifications against caring for anyone, Jenny could only speculate about its nature. Reluctant to undermine what they were building by declaring her feelings for him, she decided not to push.

Meanwhile, Brian Ladreau had been turned loose by Ned, and he was doing an excellent job as the Balfour Beach's manager. Ned's final cluster of villas on the bluff at the far end of the cove was almost complete. Simultaneously, a great many matters related to Balfour Shipping awaited his attention in London. And Oliver was getting tired. It was time for them to go.

Whenever she thought of returning to England, Jenny suffered from mixed emotions. On the one hand, she was eager to make a life with Andrew and Ned, and thoroughly smitten by the idea of looking for a town house for them to share. Yet she was reluctant to leave St. Lucia and the airy nineteenth-century house she'd begun to think of as her own. Her sojourn on the island had been near magical, a sea change of the first magnitude, and she didn't want its spell to fade.

She was also very nervous over the prospect of seeing Milo again. The old proverb, "out of sight, out of mind" was probably true in reverse as well, and she feared associating with his brother again would dredge up feelings in Ned she'd rather he would forget.

If she needed evidence that, juxtaposed with her most grievous error in judgment to date, the animosity between brothers could affect her relationship with her husband, she had only to recall Ned's strong reaction to the telegram Milo had sent after Andrew's birth. Innocuous as it had seemed, the mere fact that Milo had sent it had rubbed Ned the wrong way.

Thanks to her own reticence, she couldn't blame him for feeling as he did. Embarrassed, she'd never told him the truth about how she'd gotten pregnant. No doubt he thought she and Milo had conducted a full-blown affair.

When Christmas was just a week away, they began packing their things. In five days, they'd be taking off for London. There were numerous goodbyes to be said. Ned had proposed they entertain two Bank of England officials, David Montrose and Bradley Coates-Jeffords, and their wives at dinner as a farewell gesture. Stationed in Castries, the officials had been instrumental in arranging the resort's financing. He wanted to foster a cordial working relationship between them and the Ladreaus, who'd also be attending.

As Jenny put on a flattering emerald-green silk sheath that evening for the party, the lime-and-ginger glazed pork roast that would be her menu's pièce de résistance perfumed the air with its mouth-watering aroma.

Checked on periodically by Arabella as Jenny dressed, Andrew was nestled securely in his molded plastic baby chair atop a blanket in the living room. Ned, who'd come home a half hour late after cleaning up some last-minute details, was humming and splashing in the shower. All was right with her world.

The shower shut off as she fastened pearl studs in her ears before her pedestal-mounted mirror. A moment later, Ned came to stand behind her, a bath towel wrapped around his hips. His hair sticking in damp points to his forehead, he nuzzled a kiss against her neck.

"That roast smells wonderful," he murmured, the glint in his eyes reflecting back at her. "But then so do you. What do you say we ring our guests and beg off until spring?"

As of the previous afternoon, they'd begun to plan a May vacation on the island so Ned could supervise the construction of a spa and health club at the resort. Though she'd been looking forward to the dinner party, Jenny had to admit she'd like nothing better than to cancel it and make love to him.

"You know we can't," she responded, dimpling. "But all isn't lost. If you're game, we can excuse ourselves for a quickie between the main course and the dessert."

The slight deepening of the grooves at the corners of Ned's mouth acknowledged he knew she was only teasing him. Nevertheless, his expressive dark eyes had taken on their smoky look. His readiness for something more than sexual banter protruding beneath his towel, he spun her around to face him.

"You know damn well you're the only dessert I need," he growled as he took full possession of her mouth.

Plumbing her moist privacy with his tongue, he pictured himself making love to her in the half bath off the downstairs hall while their guests chatted unawares in the dining room. The imagined incongruity of the situation heated him to the core. From a celibate, I've become insatiable where she's concerned, he thought. I can't seem to get enough of her.

Lord, what he can make me feel! Jenny was thinking. It's as if he throws a switch only *he* knows how to manipulate. One kiss and she was crying out with need down to her toes.

Running his hands over her curves, Ned thought he heard Arabella admit someone downstairs. Had their guests arrived early? Or was it the baby-sitter? Either way, they were cutting things rather close.

Releasing Jenny, he gave her derriere a friendly pat. "Mind going downstairs and covering for me?" he asked. "I've got to get dressed and, with you in my arms, I'm not likely to get much further than dropping this towel."

Lightly caressing his hair-roughened chest with her fingertips, she paused to repair her lipstick and pat her hair into place before doing as he asked. I'm so happy, she thought, intoxicated by the quality of their closeness as she started down the stairs. Though in the past I've been something of a pessimist about male-female relationships, I'm beginning to believe that, when we return to London, everything will work out.

Absorbed in her contented musings and concomitant thoughts about checking on the table setting, at first she didn't see the lanky, fair-haired man who was squatting on his haunches by Andrew's baby chair, tickling him under the chin. A second later, she focused. And felt the bottom drop out of her safe, precious world.

What was *Milo* doing in their living room?

Glancing up at her light footsteps and gasp of indrawn breath, Ned's brother got to his feet. In his beige silk-and-wool suit, which had the look of Savile

Row about it, he was as striking as ever. And just as mocking, she guessed. She hated the very sight of him.

"*Hel*lo, Jenny," he greeted her, nonchalantly inspecting her from her shining, casual hairdo to the open toes of her spiky sandals. "I must say motherhood agrees with you. You're curvier in all the right places."

The casual, almost taunting words pierced her to the quick. How dare he speak to me that way? she demanded in silent outrage. I won't have him *touching* Andrew. Or spoiling things for me with Ned. She was so furious that, for several seconds, she was speechless.

From the dining room, where she was putting several last-minute touches to the dinner table, Arabella gave Jenny an apprehensive look. "I wanted to call you, missus," she said. "But he tol' me not to. That he's Mr. Ned's brother. He say it's all right...."

A tight feeling in her chest, Jenny assured the housekeeper she'd done nothing wrong. "Please... check on the roast to make sure it isn't burning," she requested in a shaken voice.

There was nothing shaken about her determination to resist whatever Milo was planning. As she turned back to face him, her hands were balled into fists.

"What are you doing here?" she asked indignantly. "I can't remember either of us inviting you."

Milo shrugged, projecting the self-deprecating, charming facade she remembered so well.

"This is Balfour property," he reminded her. "And I'm a Balfour family member. In answer to your question, Father decided I ought to get a handle on the company's world-wide operations so that in future I'd be more help to Ned. My travels were scheduled to commence shortly after Christmas. However, I was anxious to meet my son. And I preferred to do it away from the ancestral setting. So, I flew down early."

His assertion about the baby touched a nerve. "Andrew's not your son!" Jenny exclaimed. "You abandoned us!"

Following her deepest maternal instincts, she released the baby from his chair and scooped him up in her arms. Ned came downstairs in his dinner jacket and black tie a minute later to find them squared off like combatants. As Jenny had been before him, he was thoroughly shocked to see his brother.

Though *she* was clearly upset by Milo's presence, for Ned, seeing Jenny with him was similar to being punched in the stomach. Unwanted images filled his head—devastating mental tableaux of how they must have looked in each other's arms. Inevitably the memory of going home and finding Ronnie in bed with his ne'er-do-well sibling returned to haunt him.

A mask of control descending over his features, he asked the same basic question Jenny had. And got the same reply.

"Jenny informs me Andrew isn't my son," Milo added. "No doubt despite your knowledge of how he was conceived you agree with her. That doesn't change my strong interest in him. At the very least, I'm his uncle. And your brother. In the cause of family unity, you can hardly send me packing from your door."

Though Ned hated to admit it, Milo had a point. If Andrew was to have any sense of family connectedness, holidays and family occasions at Longwood would be part of their lives when they returned to London. Somehow, they'd have to put the issue of

Milo's paternity to rest. He just hoped he could deal with his own emotions.

Out of the corner of his eye, he saw the Montroses' midnight-blue BMW pull up at their front steps. Since they lived near each other atop the Morne, they and the Coates-Jeffords had probably driven down together. They'd be at the door in a minute. Unless he wanted a full-blown family argument to erupt in front of them, he'd have to put a lid on things.

"We'll talk about this after dinner," he told Milo shortly, avoiding Jenny's anguished gaze. "In the meantime, you're welcome to stay if you like. It goes without saying that I shall expect you to be on your best behavior."

Jenny had seen their guests arriving, too. In light of Ned's failure to extend any solidarity to her, or even to consult her before inviting Milo to dine with them, she couldn't bear to face their company without composing herself.

Snatching up Andrew's chair and blanket with her free hand as she clutched the baby to her bosom, she ran upstairs without a word to either brother. Maybe it wasn't good form to leave Ned in the lurch with guests arriving. But she had more pressing matters to think about.

With one disastrous stroke, everything they'd shared had been placed in jeopardy. Instead of opening himself further to their relationship Ned would close up like a clamshell. He'd focus on what he doubtless believed had been her dalliance with his brother and speculate that it might happen again. She winced as she recalled his injunction in setting forth the terms of their marriage that she not cuckold him with Milo.

Meanwhile she couldn't bear to let Milo have any-thing to do with Andrew. If he tried to sue for joint custody, she'd oppose him to the death.

"Oh, Andrew," she whispered, kissing her son's soft cheek as she placed him with his teddy bear in the playpen Ned had bought for him. "What are we go-ing to do? *You* know who your daddy is...just as I know which brother I love!"

If only Ned would love her in return—help her fight Milo instead of withdrawing from her—she'd feel more secure. Instinct warned he probably wouldn't. She was far from tranquil a few minutes later when Cecie Ladreau's thirteen-year-old cousin, whom they'd hired to baby-sit during the meal, arrived and came upstairs.

With Emily Ladreau on hand to care for the baby, Jenny had no excuse not to join the party. Everyone was laughing and talking over cocktails in the living room when she went back downstairs. Greeting their guests with a smile that felt pasted on her face, she excused herself to check on dinner just as quickly as she could.

In her absence Ned had asked Arabella to set an ex-tra place. To Jenny's chagrin, the housekeeper had positioned it to the right of hers. When they sat down to eat, the man who'd overwhelmed her defenses and planted the seed of a child in her became a fixture of her peripheral vision. Despite the delicious aromas that wafted from Arabella's exquisitely prepared spe-cialties, she could smell his cloying after-shave. His hands were just inches from hers.

Refusing to look at him, Jenny hoped the Ladreaus and Ned's banker friends wouldn't notice her ani-mosity toward his brother and mistake it for common rudeness. Considering the way he'd distanced himself from her, she'd have avoided eye contact with Ned, too, if she could. It wasn't to be. As the host and her dinner partner, he was seated directly across from her. She could read displeasure in his every line and aspect.

Again and again, as if in some excruciating dance, their gazes met and then slid apart. The rigid way she was ignoring Milo caused Ned's uncertainty about her motives to deepen. There's a simple explanation for the way she's acting, he tried to tell himself. She's embarrassed about their past together. And upset with him for demanding recognition as Andrew's father.

The devil's advocate in him hinted at a far different scenario. Maybe she's still in love with Milo, it suggested. And regrets the bargain she made with you.

Jenny's uninhibited response to his lovemaking was the only bulwark he possessed against such thoughts. Until proven wrong, he'd do his best to cling to it. I won't have him sleeping under the same roof with us, he vowed. The first thing I'll do when everyone leaves is phone room reservations. And the second will be to have things out with him.

When at last their guests had gone though Milo remained, drinking Ned's brandy, Jenny fled upstairs to nurse her child. As she curled up with Andrew on the window seat in her room, she could hear her husband's bass and Milo's less resonant tones in the living room. A moment later, they moved outside to the porch. Mercifully, perhaps, she couldn't make out what they were saying.

Gazing at the panoramic view of Vigie and the entrance to Castries harbor that spread out before them, the brothers watched the running lights of an aging prop plane wink against the darkness as it settled in for a landing.

"This place doesn't change much, does it?" Milo remarked.

Determined to deal with the issues of paternity and loyalty his brother's arrival had raised, Ned decided to take things slowly. He sat down on the swing before answering. "Actually I think there've been quite a few changes as a result of my efforts," he said.

His mouth twisting slightly, Milo shrugged. "You're right, of course. But they're nothing to those that have taken place in your wife. She's positively alluring these days, isn't she? One might even say radiant. Motherhood has made a real woman of her."

Despite his resolve not to let their discussion get off on the wrong foot, Ned saw red. "In my opinion," he ground out, "Jennifer has always *been* a real woman...one whose warmth and personal strength you failed to appreciate while you had the chance."

Milo appraised Ned with narrowed eyes as he leaned against the balustrade. "I do believe you've fallen in love with her," he said at last.

About to deny it, Ned wondered suddenly if he was guilty as charged. To be perfectly honest, his feelings for Jenny *had* all the earmarks....

Seemingly aware he'd thrown his powerful sibling off balance, Milo delivered a follow-up punch. "Be that as it may," he added, "since my breakup with Pam, I've cleaned up my act...given up gambling and cut back considerably on the booze. I want my son. Practically speaking, that means getting Jenny back. Under the circumstances, I consider your marriage to her a farce. I give you fair warning...I intend to go after them."

"Like hell you will!"

Heartsick because he didn't know where Jenny stood and so angry he couldn't see straight, Ned suppressed an urge to indulge in physical violence. Yet the swing bumped violently against the side of the house as he got to his feet.

"Get out of my house," he ordered after a moment, controlling himself with difficulty. "And stay out. Andrew's my son and I don't intend to relinquish him. As for Jennifer, since the baby was born, she's been my wife in every sense of the word. As such, she's entitled to my protection."

On the surface, at least, Milo didn't seem perturbed by the thinly veiled threat. "Your wishes in this matter don't mean a damn to me," he said. "I'm interested in what Jenny thinks. I sweet-talked her once, and I can do it again."

Ned didn't reply and, with a little salute, Milo set his empty glass on the railing and sauntered down the front steps, heading toward the hotel where, in all probability, he'd left his luggage with the concierge.

So angry he'd thought it possible he might kill his brother if he laid a hand on him, Ned finished his drink and went into the living room to pour another at the liquor cart. Downing it neat, he pocketed the cigarettes and disposable lighter David Montrose had left behind.

He needed to get out of the house before he smashed something. Or made a fool of himself by begging Jenny to honor her promise to him. We shouldn't have become lovers, he thought, going back outside and walking down the front steps to cross the road and sit on the low wall, which overlooked the beach. Not without settling some things first.

He hadn't smoked in several years, having given it up for his health. The urge to do so now was overwhelming. Lighting up, he inhaled deeply.

What he needed was a plan. And, in essence, he had one. Though he'd fight to keep his son, his pride wouldn't let him pressure the woman who'd brought him so much bliss. If she stayed with him, it would have to be voluntary. They hadn't talked about feelings and the sad truth was he couldn't predict what path she'd take.

Distraught and increasingly concerned when Ned didn't come to bed, Jenny put the baby in his cradle and returned to the window seat. Looking toward the beach, she spotted the firefly glow of her husband's cigarette. His back to the house, he was staring out over the water.

She'd never seen him smoke before. That he would do so now only underscored how upset he was. Ned, *trust* me! she wanted to shout. I'd never shame you with your brother. With all the love that was in her heart, she longed to run to him.

Instead of seeking her out and insisting they talk, he'd retreated into his shell. She didn't feel as if she had the right to intrude. Praying she'd know what to say or do if he gave her the chance, she got into bed to wait for him.

Chapter Twelve

Though Jenny managed to stay awake for hours, Ned never did come to bed. Around 2:45 a.m., she finally fell asleep. She didn't stir when, shortly afterward, he came upstairs and paused a moment in her open doorway before going into the next room.

More exhausted than refreshed, she was having coffee on the porch in her robe the following morning when she saw him and Brian go by in the Jeep. Though he glanced in her direction, he didn't wave. Is this how it's going to be from now on? she wondered. A chasm of unarticulated feelings widening between us each time Milo shows his face?

It occurred to her that Ned's disagreeable, self-centered brother was probably still on the island, primed to create more trouble for them. She'd be a sitting duck there in the house if he decided to come looking for her. No way am I ever going to be his victim again, she thought. Abandoning her coffee and an untouched cinnamon bun to the sugar birds, she went into the house to dress.

"Andrew's been fed," she informed Arabella, appearing in the kitchen doorway a few minutes later in shorts, a printed T-shirt and rubber beach thongs. "I've put him into his chair in the living room. I'm going for a walk, and I'll need you to look after him for a little while. Under no circumstances is Mr. Ned's brother to come near him. Understood?"

Wide-eyed, Arabella nodded.

"If Mr. Milo asks for *me,*" Jenny added, "tell him I've gone into town and won't be back for several hours. Ask him to return when Mr. Ned's at home."

The housekeeper nodded again. "Yes, Mrs. Jen."

"Okay, then."

Plagued by a strong sense of urgency she couldn't quite define, Jenny went out and headed down the steps to the beach. She was avoiding Milo and she guessed he probably wouldn't come looking for her there. From what she knew of him, he was the type to sip something alcoholic in a comfortable chair, not a dedicated jogger and swimmer like her husband. Besides, if she was to find the right words to convince Ned his brother meant nothing to her and beg him to help her keep Milo away from their son, she needed time alone, to think. Since arriving on St. Lucia, she'd considered the beach a perfect place for soul-searching.

Unknown to her as she'd crossed the narrow ribbon of blacktop that separated their house from the low stone wall where Ned had smoked and pondered the night before, Milo had been approaching the house on foot. He'd just gained the little rise several hundred yards down the road. Glimpsing her, he'd changed course and accelerated his pace. Before much time had passed, he was descending the steps to the beach in hot pursuit.

After completing their tour of unfinished projects around the resort complex, Ned had dropped Brian at his hotel office. Instead of buzzing up to the point to check on the last of the completed villas as planned, he continued to sit in the Jeep under the canopy of the hotel's porte cochere, staring into space.

You're behaving like a dunce, he castigated himself. Nothing Jen has ever said or done, with the possible exception of that time she asked about Milo's baby pictures, could be construed as a declaration of love for him. Or even liking. Meanwhile, she's been your willing partner in every sensual escapade you've proposed. She's treated you with warmth, affection and respect.

If he wanted to know how Jenny felt about him versus his brother, the thing to do was *ask*. Shifting gears, he roared up the bluff to the house and parked with a jolt in his usual spot. Scheduled to stay on and keep house for Oliver and Viv when they vacationed on the island in January, Arabella was polishing furniture in the living room when he walked in through the front door.

"Where's Mrs. Jen?" he demanded urgently.

The housekeeper gave him an uncomfortable look. "She went walkin' on the beach, Mr. Ned. I think maybe your brother jus' went down there after her."

His mouth compressed in a forbidding line, Ned pushed back out the door. By God, he'd see for himself what was going on. Given his objective, the wall across the road turned out to be the ideal vantage point. He reached it just in time to see Jenny standing at the waterline several hundred yards down the beach, her hair whipping in the breeze and her hearing almost certainly impaired by the crash of the breakers as Milo approached her from behind. He winced as his brother put both arms around her.

If Jenny was going to respond to Milo's overtures, even for a second, Ned realized he didn't want to know about it. The memory would forever poison their relationship for him, whether they continued as lovers or returned to the polite but stilted marriage of convenience he'd first proposed.

Stifling an urge to show up on the beach and resolve matters with his fists, Ned returned to the house. In the living room, Andrew had begun to fuss and Arabella was jiggling him against her shoulder. God but he loved his little son! *And* Jenny. He had to admit it: Milo had shown amazing insight.

Dropping a kiss on the baby's head, he went upstairs to the room he'd occupied the night before and tried to think. By appealing to Jenny's sense of fairness and decency, he knew, he could keep her. Regrettably, now that he'd discovered how much he loved her, mere possession wasn't enough.

He wanted to be the man enthroned in her heart, the lover she meshed with so perfectly that in ways he'd just begun to understand they'd be like one person. Commitment and caring that way didn't come because you begged for them. They were given freely, or not at all. Maybe I should go somewhere overnight, he thought. Give her enough time and privacy to decide what she really wants.

On the beach, Jenny had wrenched free of Milo's embrace. "How dare you touch me... you who, in effect, raped me after plying me with alcohol?'' she'd raged.

And got me pregnant. Her unspoken accusation had been like a knife, flashing in the salt-laden air between them.

Milo shrugged. ''You seem happy enough with the result.''

''If you mean Andrew, I love him more than life itself. And don't try to tell me you feel the same way. For all you cared, he could have been suctioned from my womb in some abortion clinic. Or handed over to adoptive parents.''

''He's my son,'' Milo insisted with a stab at what with him, she guessed, passed for sincerity. ''I want him back. And you, Jenny. You were crazy about me once. You could be again. I admit Ned was right when he said I didn't appreciate your sterling qualities. I've come to my senses, and I want to take care of you and the baby. We belong together. If you'll give me another chance....''

Ned said that about me? Jenny asked herself in amazement. *When?* Last night, when I thought he'd thrown up his wall again, was he actually still within reach? Something softened in her eyes at the thought and Milo misinterpreted it. He tried to take her in his arms again.

''No!'' she protested, pushing him away with all her strength. ''If you don't stop manhandling me, I'll report you to the police. I want to know what you're trying to pull by coming down here and upsetting everyone. In my experience, you're concerned with the good of just one person . . . yourself. You don't give a damn about Andrew and me. Not *really.* So, why do you want us? To hurt Ned? Or win points with Oliver

by taking credit for the grandchild he's always wanted?''

The look on Milo's face told her she'd hit pay dirt on both counts. For once, he didn't have a ready answer.

''You're disgusting,'' she told him. ''A worm compared with your brother, whom I happen to love. You're *never* going to get me back. Or Andrew. If you want my advice, you'll get out of St. Lucia fast...hop a plane for anyplace handy before I tell my husband you tried to put a move on me and he comes after you.''

Returning to the house, Jenny saw Ned's Jeep parked outside. He was there, at the exact moment she needed him! Yet the minute she walked in the door she could tell from Arabella's face that something was amiss.

''Where's Mr. Ned?'' she asked with a tingle of apprehension.

The housekeeper rolled her eyes and gestured toward the stairs. ''In his room, missus.''

Andrew's fussing clearly indicated he wanted to be nursed, but Jenny didn't pause. She found Ned stuffing articles of clothing into an overnight bag. ''Where are you going?'' she blurted, a spurt of panic causing her pulse to race.

Despite her strong conviction that he was deeply upset, his features were as blank and expressionless as a beach where a hurricane has passed when he turned to face her. ''I saw you and Milo together a few minutes ago,'' he admitted tonelessly. ''And I...''

Jenny felt sick to her stomach. ''Nothing happened...no thanks to your brother!'' she insisted, praying he'd believe her. "He tried to kiss me and I told him to get lost. That's absolutely all there was to it."

Though Ned took considerable comfort in her words, in his view the larger picture was anything but clear. The fact that Jenny had rejected Milo didn't mean she wasn't still in love with him. Like the original terms of their marriage, those of Ned's sexual *rapprochement* with her revolved around convenience. His hedging of bets the night they'd first made love had come back to haunt him with a vengeance.

"I appreciate your loyalty," he told her in a strangled voice. "All the same, I've decided to clear out overnight . . . give you time to decide what you really want."

She realized in a flash of intuition that he didn't have a clue to how she felt. For a tough, intelligent, practical man, Ned Balfour could be an incredible fool. "I don't *need* time," she said. "As for what I want . . ."

Enmeshed in his private thoughts, Ned wasn't really listening to her. "Last night," he revealed, "after you went upstairs to nurse the baby, Milo informed me he'd gotten his act together. He claims to have stopped gambling and eased up on the alcohol. He wants you back, Jen. And Andrew. He wants to make a life for you."

"And you plan to let him take us? Without a fight?"

By now hot tears were streaming down Jenny's cheeks. In response, Ned swore. Abandoning his task, he gripped her painfully by the shoulders. "Can't you see I don't *want* to?" he asked. "That I love you, damn it, with everything that's in my soul to give? The fact is, I'm not the sort of man who can be with a woman, yet wonder if she..."

"Ned, you *dolt!*" Obviating the need for an explanation, Jenny flung her arms around his neck.

He blinked. "Jen, does this mean..."

She was smiling at him through her tears. "I love you, too," she whispered. "I have ever since the night we danced together at the jump-up. Maybe even before. As for wanting you, I've craved you shamefully from the moment I saw you drying off that afternoon on your boat."

It was as if he'd been handed the earth. And the moon and stars to go with it. Jenny loved him. Shutting his eyes at the improbable splendor of it, he bent his head and claimed her with a kiss.

It was midmorning and they were fully clothed. He wasn't inside her the way they both suddenly longed for him to be. Yet the sublime explosion of desire and trust, of male demand and female receptivity, swiftly took them deeper than they'd known it was possible to go.

In a way that was as primitive as the earth, yet as new as their willingness to reveal themselves, they'd fused. Henceforth, neither would be alone in the world. Though they could have survived without each other, together they'd *live.*

"I want you...now," Ned confessed, drawing back a little to caress her mouth with one loving finger.

"And I want you."

Unfortunately for passion, the door to the hall stood open. Arabella was tapping lightly and respectfully against the door frame. "You want me to take the laundry over to the washhouse now, missus?" she asked with a broad smile when she got their attention. "Or..."

If Arabella was at the washhouse, she couldn't be caring for Andrew so they could make love. "Clean sheets can wait, Arabella," Ned answered firmly, preempting Jenny. "As soon as Andrew's fed, you'll be needed to baby-sit."

As it turned out, their son was more cranky than hungry. With a minimum of nursing, he was content. While Jenny changed him and put him down for a nap, Ned phoned his secretary.

"Tell Brian we'll be using honeymoon suite A on the point this afternoon and that we're not to be disturbed," he ordered. "And I mean by *anyone*... with the sole exception of our housekeeper. As of this moment, any touch-up work still going on at the villas is to cease."

They were off in the Jeep a few minutes later. Honeymoon suite A, which still smelled slightly of fresh paint, had the kind of bed Jenny'd always dreamed about. A whimsical, wrought-iron four-poster with filmy mosquito curtains, it was lavished with white-on-white cutwork embroidered sheets and a resplendence of pillows.

Nick inserted his hands beneath her shirt to caress her slender ribcage and soft, full breasts. "What do you say we disarrange it?" he suggested.

"Yes. Oh, *yes*..." Jenny answered, her fingers separating his buttons from their buttonholes.

He was hers, now, this blunt, powerful yet surprisingly vulnerable man—to undress, to love, to cherish all her days. Just as she was his. His erect, unabashed seeking belonged to both of them. So did her moist sheath and the bud of her arousal. Convenience wasn't remotely a part of the bright, self-immolating yet healing tapestry they would weave together.

A moment later, he'd tugged her T-shirt over her head. She'd pushed his shirt back from his shoulders and down his arms. Zipper teeth rasped faintly as their shorts were shed, to be followed by his briefs and her bikini panties.

Pacing them, though he was wild to bursting, Ned stroked her nipples through her bra's lacy cups before separating its front clasp. As her breasts spilled into his hands, she grasped him and drew him toward her emptiness. He grunted with pleasure. With him tucked tightly between her legs, they swayed, rubbing against each other.

The bed was everything Jenny could want. Yet just past the sliding glass doors, a blue wilderness of private clifftop plunge pool and iridescent, sun-drenched sea beckoned. In just four days, they'd return to the cold, gray drizzle of winter in England.

"I know what I said," she told Ned breathlessly between soft, biting kisses. "But it would be...so *wonderful*...to love you out there...."

He caught fire with the idea in an instant. Maintaining a bridge of touch, they stepped naked onto the flagstones of the pool apron. The air was warm, the breeze soft, the pool's water heated per Ned's instructions prior to the inspection tour he'd planned.

He'd shown Jenny the villas before, just after the plunge pools had been constructed. But it was only as they descended into the shallow end of the particular pool awaiting them that she realized the utility of its freestanding underwater seats.

They'd be able to join comfortably in the water with her astride his lap. Ablaze with need, Jenny straddled the man she loved, drawing him deep with her strong interior muscles as he entered her, and wrapping her arms around him.

From the blind look on his face, she knew he was struggling for control. Achieving it, he began to move—not in great, shuddering thrusts the way he sometimes did, but with a suppressed rhythm and intensity that were all the more impassioned for their forced containment. Waves of longing crested, broke over them and created again.

"I have all of you," Ned asserted in a low growl, blatantly thumbing her nipples as they drowned in each other's eyes.

"The way I have you."

A diffused glow kindled by the fullness of him in her most private places caused the circles of Jenny's excitement to widen until she thought they must encompass the universe.

She wouldn't be able to say, later, how long they conjured there in the sparkling air, with the wavelets they stirred up rocking like tender love slaps against their skin, only that the fusion they sought erased the last of their boundaries as it lifted them higher than she'd ever thought they could go.

Ultimately they reached their peak. Jenny broke free first, crying out in little bleats of ecstasy as the most implosive shudders she'd ever experienced took her. Ned followed in seconds, a fierce sheen of gooseflesh spreading over his back and legs.

They were welded tightly to each other as satisfaction permeated muscle and bone. Milo's gone, whether or not he took my advice and left the island, Jenny thought, when coherence was possible again. So is the separateness of our past. From this day forward, we'll only move deeper, live more closely together.

Tranquil at last, they moved to the deep end of the pool to talk of things that, in retrospect, didn't seem to matter that much. Trust made the words come easily.

"There's something I want you to know," Jenny began, tracing the little groove beside Ned's mouth.

He kissed her fingertips. "Tell me."

"Milo and I didn't have an affair...not the way you must think. I never loved him. Or even thought I did. We dated for a few weeks, that's all. It was nice to have a native Britisher escort me around London. He showed me nothing but charm and deference until one evening in his flat when he plied me with champagne."

"You mean..."

She nodded. "What happened between us wasn't voluntary on my part. I'm not used to drinking a great deal of alcohol, and it hit me pretty hard. When he pushed me down on his living-room couch and tore off my panties, I tried to fight him. But I couldn't make him stop. I'd never been with a man before and I was literally terrified."

Briefly her eyes grew shadowed at the recollection.

Shocked and infuriated past belief, Ned was ready to do murder on her behalf. Milo had taken Jenny's virginity in addition to impregnating her. "I'll kill him!" he swore, his jaw and powerful fists clenching. "Make him pay for what he did..."

"No." Jenny laid her cheek against his, cooling it. "Because of his crudity, his utter selfishness, we have Andrew. And each other. Milo himself has become irrelevant."

Pushing down anger, particularly an anger so justified and intrinsic to his cherished role as Jenny's protector didn't come easy to Ned despite the iron control he'd exercised the night before. For her sake, he'd make the attempt.

"As long as we're sharing secrets," he said gruffly after a moment, "I have one for you, too. My motives in coming up with the asinine concept of a marriage without love or emotional commitment sprang from another of Milo's escapades. My first wife, Veronica, and I had been married slightly more than a year when I came home to our Kensington flat several hours early one afternoon and found them in bed together."

It was Jenny's turn to feel shock and dismay as the last stones of Ned's bastion tumbled. "I can scarcely believe it," she said after a moment, shaking her head in amazement. "With you for her husband, what can she have been thinking of?"

So sincere, so obviously lacking in calculation, the compliment consigned whatever sense of inadequacy and victimization Ned had left to the scrap heap. Jenny loved him. It was enough. Simply by being the woman she was, she'd taught him how to trust again.

"You know," he remarked, kissing the tip of her nose, "I have only one reason left to be jealous of my brother."

Jenny's delicate brows drew together in a frown. "Surely you don't feel that way now that we..."

"Though it happened by accident, Milo had the privilege of giving you a child."

To her relief, she realized he'd spoken rhetorically—with love, not envy.

"Oh, Ned..." Desire curling back to life inside her, she grasped his buttocks and drew him close. "Haven't you realized yet that, when Andrew's a little older, I'll want you to give me another baby?"

The thought fired his imagination and abruptly he was ready for another round. Before things got too hot and heavy, one last confidence needed to be exchanged.

"Nothing would make me happier, sweetheart," he admitted. "But you know what? No matter how many children we have, Andrew will always be first in my heart."

Tears of gratitude for the wonder that he was pricked Jenny's eyelids. Andrew was indescribably precious to her, too. "Why do you say that?" she asked.

Ned's reply was muffled against her mouth. "Because *he's* the one who brought us together."

* * * * *

Take 4 bestselling love stories FREE

Plus get a FREE surprise gift!

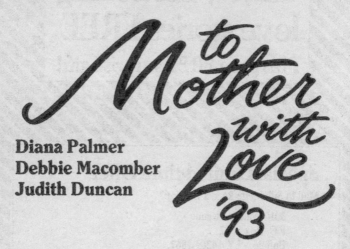 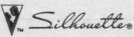